MW00936565

The Ransom

KIERA CHAREST

ISBN-10: 1721157557
ISBN-13: 978-1721157556

To my siblings, Mikaela and Jacob

Prologue

The Great Hall sparkled in the torchlight as a queen sat regally upon her throne. Knights, nobles and ladies filled the room, creating an ever present chatter around the Hall. A pope in white robes stood to the right of the queen.

A sudden fanfare filled the air, stilling the pleasant talk throughout the room. The queen stood and turned her attention to the big oak doors across from her. The doors were opened and a young baron, the queen's age, entered, followed by a steward. The steward melted into the crowd and allowed the noble to continue down the aisle alone.

The queen let out a nervous breath as the lord took his stand next to her. She glanced up in hopes of seeing how he felt. He seemed completely calm. The young woman rubbed her hands together and rung them fervently. The lord seemed to take notice and glanced down at her with intense blue eyes. He gave her a reassuring smile and took her hand, rubbing it with gentleness, and sending a comforting shiver down the queen's back. The queen responded with a smile and they both turned to face the pope. The crowd watched as the pope approached the two nobles.

"My queen, would you please kneel?" the pope began.

The queen released the baron's hand and sank to her knees in obedience.

The pope ordered the lord to do the same before turning to the queen once again. "Do you, my great queen, solemnly swear to continue to protect your kingdom from danger?"

"Yes," the queen's voice called out, without waver.

"Do you still wish me to continue with this ceremony and make this baron your husband and king to this kingdom?"

The gathering waited for their queen to answer. The woman bent her head and replied, "Yes, I wish you to do so."

The pope turned to the young noble beside her. "Do you, my lord, wish me to continue and coronate you to the position of king?"

"Yes, I do," the lord replied.

"And do you wish me to make you the husband of our beloved queen?"

This time the woman waited for the noble's voice.

"Yes, I do," the baron's voice called out through the Hall.

"Then, I ask you to solemnly swear to protect and serve your kingdom in every breath you take until your last."

"I swear," the noble's voice announced in determination.

The pope took a glittering golden crown filled with precious jewels and placed it upon the baron's head. "May you rule with strength and wisdom that the good Lord gives you. Hereby, lords and ladies, I give to you your new king and his wife, the queen of the great kingdom of Aurum. Rise both of you and may you live forever, protecting your kingdom even in the face of death."

The queen and the newly made king rose to a standing position as cheers erupted from the gathered nobility. The queen smiled in response, unsure of what to make of her new life as a wife and secondary leader. She had ruled for four years without the help of a king. What was there to do when you no longer held the upper hand of authority?

The young king glanced at his new wife and observed her serene disposition. But he knew better. Her striking green eyes told him it was all an act. Beneath, there was an uncomfortable and nervous state of mind. He took her hand like he had in the beginning and rubbed it gently, trying to calm her.

He could still hear the pope's words echo throughout his mind. *"Solemnly swear to protect your kingdom...may you live forever, protecting your kingdom even in the face of death."*

His hand slipped from the queen's and came to rest around her waist. He pulled her to him in a protective manner and whispered words for her ears only, "And I solemnly swear to protect you, my love, even in the face of death. I've vowed to do so ever since I was a squire."

Chapter 1

2 years later...

A chilling cry broke through the cold winter morning. Charlotte tore up the spiral stairs following the desperate cries towards her solar. The cries carried on echoing off the cold stone walls. Reaching the solar door, she shoved it open. Her close friend, Alice, stood by the fireplace, rocking a bundle back and forth, shushing as she swayed. Alice's four year old daughter, Faye, sat on the floor, observing a wooden toy horse. Alice looked up at Charlotte and smiled, "Good day, my queen, I take it you heard the princess?"

She let out a sigh of relief at the comforting sight. Smiling she reached out for her daughter, "Could I see my little child?"

Alice walked over to Charlotte ever so gently and handed the baby girl over, "Here's your mother, Princess Myla," she cooed. Myla began to whimper again and Charlotte walked around the room, carefully rocking her baby girl to sleep. Myla's intense blue eyes fluttered shut and Charlotte came to stand by Alice once again. Alice flicked the sleeping child's ebony hair from her closed eyes. "I can't believe how much she's grown," Alice commented. "She'll be a year tomorrow." Alice looked at Charlotte, "You must be proud to have brought your child this far."

Charlotte nodded, "I am. I was nervous about losing her to some strange sickness or the epidemic. But the Lord has shown mercy."

"Indeed He has, my queen." Alice turned her eyes to Charlotte, a smile playing on her lips, "And I daresay her father is exceptionally proud."

Charlotte felt herself blush and nodded. Her husband and king, Peter, would surely be proud. Most men would want a son to carry on the hierarchy and royal line of their kingdom. That was what had made Charlotte so nervous when she had found out she had given Peter a daughter. She had been worried Peter would be disappointed in her and his new child. Peter's reaction stunned both her and the entire royal household, who had been praying for Charlotte to give the king a son. Instead of disappointment, Peter had been greatly pleased at his new child and had spared no effort in making sure everyone knew it. With each passing day, Peter seemed to grow closer and closer to Myla. He had made it his duty to see Myla every day, despite his busy schedule. On top of that, Peter found it fitting to spoil his little girl beyond measure. Charlotte would never have thought Peter would turn out to be such a great father and king as well. She had thought his countless duties as ruler would take him away from her and Myla.

"Mother!" an echoed cry broke into Charlotte's thoughts.

The cry woke Myla and she began to look around for the cause of her interruption.

"Mother, I'm back!" the cry came again.

Charlotte recognized the voice to be Alice's oldest boy, Gavin.

"Gavin!" another call answered. That was the steward, Alice's husband, Rowan. "Do not shout so, for you'll wake Princess Myla," Rowan scolded. Ever since Peter had become king he had requested that Rowan and his family be moved from the serf's village and into the castle grounds to serve the royal family. Rowan was the steward, Alice was Myla's nurse as well as Charlotte's new handmaid and Gavin would soon be Charlotte's Page.

A chuckle rang out from the hall. Charlotte recognized the voice to be Peter's. "Do not scold the boy so, Rowan. He wouldn't have wakened little Myla. I heard her crying from downstairs."

Gavin came barging in, causing Myla to whimper and snuggle closer to Charlotte's chest.

"Gavin," Alice began, "please take care to knock next time. Do you really believe the queen will approve of such behavior from a page?"

Charlotte jounced Myla up and down, "It's alright, Alice. He shall learn in time. It is like the king said, Myla was already awake."

"Of course," Alice replied.

At that moment, Peter came in, accompanied by Rowan. Peter's blue eyes lit up at the sight of Myla. He walked over to Charlotte and offered her a quick kiss. "My queen and little princess." He scooped Myla into his arms and began to coo as he paced around the large solar. "How is my precious little gem today?"

Charlotte smiled as the familiar scene took place again; with Peter swinging Myla up in the air and the girl returning the gesture with her sweet gurgling baby voice. She reached to take hold of Peter's fingers which he willingly gave her to grasp. Peter nuzzled Myla once more before returning to Charlotte's side. "Since tomorrow is Myla's first birthday, I insist upon an extravagant celebration for our little princess."

Charlotte smiled and nodded, "It is as you say, Peter. But," Charlotte added, holding up a finger, "I don't wish for you to overdo it. You know how unwise it would be to spend our treasury on a celebration."

"Very well. I will only spend the necessary amount." He handed Myla to Alice and bent to kiss Charlotte's hand, "You have my word, o great queen."

Charlotte swatted him, "Oh hush!" she responded with a tease. "Off with you now."

Peter smiled, "I will. If this celebration is going to fare as well as I want, I must get to work straight away." He bowed to Charlotte, "I will see you later, my queen." Gesturing for Rowan to follow him, Peter left the room.

Charlotte nodded. The word 'queen' didn't seem to amount to much ever since Peter had been declared king. The second he was coronated her people seemed to turn to him for leadership. Because of her desire for respect and power in her realm, Charlotte had avoided the concept of marriage for the risk of her power being stolen from her by her husband. But, knowing that she could not live forever, brought along the problem of a future heir and the kingdom's security. Many nobles would have fit the role of a king to perfection and would have been glad to marry her. But Charlotte could see right through all of them. She knew they didn't truly care about her. All they wanted was her power and riches. Charlotte refused to marry someone like that. It would only create turmoil in her peaceful kingdom. So, in order to make her subjects pleased, she turned to the only lord she truly was fond of, Peter. The young lord was the complete opposite of the other possible nobles. He was selfless and cared nothing about doubling his power and riches. He was content with what he had and never wanted more. And, there was no doubting that Peter had fallen in love with her years before. To be honest with herself,

Charlotte had begun to have affection for Peter ever since he had rescued her from Lord Roger. However, she had refused to show it, knowing it to be too dangerous. But, Peter soon proved her wrong on the matter. Since he was coronated he had allowed her to rule by his side and make decisions with him and the council.

When Myla was born however, she had to step away from her vigorous life and take care of her child. Charlotte loved Myla with all her heart but she missed the feeling of sitting upon a throne, ruling an entire kingdom. And even though Alice took most of the hard child rearing off Charlotte's hands, she still wasn't able to rule beside Peter all the time. But, in time, she knew it would be worth it. Charlotte hadn't grown up with a mother so she found it fitting that Myla spend time with her family.

Now, Peter sat on the throne and did the job for her. With Myla turning one tomorrow, perhaps Charlotte wouldn't have to stay in her solar all day, but sit beside Peter and take up her position as a powerful queen. But, she knew no matter how hard she tried, Charlotte would never have complete control over her kingdom again. Forevermore it would be a shared position.

Chapter 2

"Your Royal Highness has an ample supply of provisions for all four courses at the celebration this evening," Rowan informed. Peter walked around the Great Hall, surveying every little detail the servants had added to the room. Large garlands were being strung up across the walls. Flowers sat on the large, wooden tables. Fine, fresh greens lay upon the stone floor, waiting to perfume the room when stepped on. "And I have ordered minstrels and tumblers for the Royal family's enjoyment," Rowan continued, tagging along after Peter and enumerating the rest of the evening's events.

Movement caught Peter's eye. Turning towards the door, he saw Charlotte sweep in and inspect the Hall with narrowed eyes. Peter watched as her bright, green eyes traveled from the ceiling to the floor then back up to him. He watched her take a deep breath and start towards him. "It looks delightful so far, Peter," she complemented when she came to face him. "But," she added, "I take it you were careful of the expenses?"

Peter smiled, took her hand, and replied, "Do not worry, dear, I only supplied the necessities."

Rowan had broken off speaking and made a respectful bow to Charlotte. "My queen," he said.

Peter watched as Charlotte stiffened but nodded in response. Rowan murmured, "I shall leave you, my king," and swept away to observe a few servants carrying out orders. With Rowan distancing himself, Charlotte relaxed. Peter frowned. He had observed Charlotte over the past few days and noticed her constant restless behavior when people called her 'my queen'. Even though she covered her actions as she disguised her many moods, Peter noticed everything she did. She no longer fooled him. He could easily recognize her disturbed behavior. Perhaps it was due to not being the sole ruler. Myla's birth had kept her from the life she loved the most. She never blamed her daughter though. Charlotte loved Myla as did Peter. And he loved Charlotte even more for giving him Myla. He just needed to convince Charlotte that Myla's birth would never affect her place as queen.

Charlotte glided down the stairway, heading towards the bubble of human laughter and chatter floating from the Great Hall. Alice followed close behind with Myla in her arms. Myla, having seen little else besides the walls of Charlotte's solar and the castle gardens, was looking around wide-eyed, twisting from left to right in wonder. Charlotte smiled at Myla's curiosity. It wouldn't be long before her daughter would be exploring the castle walls for herself. Even at her young age, she was beginning to show an adventurous spirit. A porter by the Great Hall's door stepped forward when Charlotte approached. He straightened, bowed and walked ahead of Charlotte, announcing in a loud voice, "Behold, Queen Charlotte of Aurum!" The once chattering nobles and ladies stopped and turned their attention to her. Charlotte entered and observed the room in admiration. Large chandeliers illuminated the Great Hall, minstrels aligned against a wall, ready to play a rousing tune when they were allowed to rise. Charlotte raised her voice to be heard by all, "You may rise!" Nobles, ladies, minstrels, and servants stood tall and resumed their talk and orders. The minstrels started a lively tune on their lyres and lutes. The sweet aroma of lavender wafted up to her nostrils, filling them with a pleasant smell. Charlotte scanned the crowd for Peter. But her husband's face was nowhere to be seen.

Alice came to stand by her side as Sir Randolph, Peter's former instructor, approached. "My queen! You have my congratulations on Princess Myla's first year!"

Charlotte smiled and nodded, "Thank you, Sir Randolph." The knight reached over to pat Myla's dark hair. "Do you happen to know where my husband may be?"

"I'm afraid not, my queen. I haven't seen the king since the beginning of the party. Most likely he is hidden in the crowd." Sir Randolph gave Charlotte's hand a swift kiss, making her wince. She still hadn't grown used to the gesture from anyone except Peter. She covered it quickly though. As Sir Randolph melted back into the crowd, Charlotte started forward in search of Peter.

Peter stood near the newly knighted Simon, and listened to Sir Richard as he described his struggle with yet another siege attack from an ambitious young lord. "No noble has attempted this until recently. I don't understand the lord's eagerness. It's a rather sorry lot of land in the country. What could he possibly gain with such a piece of land?"

"More land than he has," Peter answered. "Land and power is what many consider the most important treasures." Which, in his opinion, was a waste of effort. What about being simply grateful for what you have? Not even under extreme circumstances would Peter ever bend to such notions.

"Have you not tried to double your guards in the country? That would surely discourage the fiery lord to leave your land in peace."

"I ordered another dispatch of soldiers to the country but I can't spare double," Sir Richard explained. "I have only so many men at my disposal. Men are scarce as it is, for I'm renting the land from Lord Edmund."

Peter nodded in understanding, "I'm sure the high lord would allow you more men if you asked."

Sir Richard shook his head, "He has stretched his men far enough. I don't want to worry him over a small matter like this. His lordship is not as young as he once was. He's getting on in years."

"You might worry him more if his lands are in peril," Peter advised. "I recommend breaking the news to Lord Edmund soon before this gets out of your control."

Sir Richard opened his mouth to reply when Simon gave a sudden bow and formal address, "My queen."

Peter turned to see Charlotte behind him. Her very image captivated him and held him spellbound. Her hair flowed to her waist in waves of ebony. Her eyes flashed with green in the sparkling torchlight and her lips were painted a glossy, rich, red. Her dress was made of a dark, uranium blue satin with tiny precious diamonds glistening off her billowing sleeves. On top of her head sat the gold and silver crown of the queen. Peter reached for her hand and guided her closer to him. "My beautiful queen," he murmured, meaning every word. A sweet squeal came from behind Charlotte. Only then did Peter notice Myla struggling in desperation to free herself from Alice's arms.

Peter chuckled and held his arms out for his daughter. Myla fell into them with gratitude and began to inspect his doublet, tugging at it in curiosity.

Simon gave Myla's hair a slight tousle, "We will leave you, my king." Making another bow to Charlotte, Sir Richard and Simon made their way towards a group of knights. Charlotte's hard gaze followed the two knights making Peter frown and observe her closely. Her eyes swam with numerous emotions. Each one at war with another.

Peter held Myla against his shoulder and shifted her over to his right side. With his left hand, he took Charlotte's palm and placed a kiss on the back of it. Charlotte jolted as if struck by lightening and whirled to face him. Peter, startled by her response, asked warily, "Charlotte?"

Seeming to compose herself, she smiled and replied, "I'm fine, Peter. You only startled me."

"I see," Peter said. She was hiding something. Her eyes told him all. But, he knew she dared not discuss something with him at a public gathering. Too many ears would be tuned to hear. Most likely the wrong ones.

"With your approval, I will leave you, my mistress." Alice hadn't mentioned a word the whole time, but had simply stood silently behind Charlotte.

Charlotte nodded, "Yes, you may be dismissed."

"Hold a moment, Alice," Peter said.

Alice stopped in her tracks and turned to face him, "Yes, my king?"

Peter placed Myla in Alice's arms, much to the princess' dismay. She began to whimper softly. Alice shushed her by rocking her back and forth. "Hold Myla for a moment." Peter pulled Charlotte to him. "I wish to dance with my queen."

Alice smiled, "Of course, Your Greatness."

At that moment, Gavin bounded up to Alice, "Mother! Can I take the princess? I want to show her and Faye something."

Alice looked to Charlotte for approval. With Charlotte's nod, Alice placed Myla in Gavin's open arms. Gavin gave an awkward bow with the bundle and bounded away the same way he'd come. Alice made a curtsy and backed towards the disappearing children, "I shall look after them, my king and queen."

After Alice had gone to follow the children, Charlotte turned back to look at Peter. He smiled and extended his palm to her, "Shall we, my queen?"

Charlotte slipped her hand into his in an uncertain fashion. Peter gave it a reassuring squeeze and swept her into the group of swaying couples. Charlotte's free hand gripped his shoulder as she cast a look around her and brought her gaze back up to his. Peter smiled into her beautiful gaze and continued to sweep her around in circles. Once she began to relax, he would broach the subject of her recent behavior. The music began to slow its pace and Peter felt Charlotte's tense muscles relax under his touch. Her head leaned forward near his chest and her breathing stilled to that of contentment. Peter stole a glance at her bowed head. Charlotte's eyes were closed and a slight smile played on the edge of her lips. Peter held her closer, her guard was beginning to fall. Soon, she would open up to him.

The song faded from the minstrels' instruments and another commenced. Peter began with the start of the new song. "Charlotte?" he asked in a soft whisper.

"Yes, Peter?"

"Do you mind if I ask you something?"

Charlotte's head left his chest and she looked up at him in puzzlement, "What do you have in mind?"

He leaned closer to her forehead, "Something that concerns me deeply."

Charlotte nodded in a slow manner, "I see." She let out an almost inaudible sigh and added, "Very well, you may ask me."

Peter drew a breath before asking. Charlotte's mood was as unpredictable as the weather. You never knew if you were to receive a storm or a warm summer day. "I've noticed lately that when people address you as 'queen' you stiffen. Why is that?"

Charlotte bowed her head, "I'm afraid it's a rather sorry answer for you to hear. I was foolish to behave so."

Peter released her waist and guided her chin up, "Please tell me, my love," he coaxed in a gentle voice.

Charlotte rested her head on his chest again and began, "I feel the status of 'queen' and the greeting 'my queen' is of little importance since you have taken the throne. I find it vexing when no one calls me 'Your Highness', 'Your

Greatness', or 'Your Majesty' any more. If they do, it is very rare."

Peter frowned, "They do not?"

Charlotte's head snapped up, "Of course not. They save the more flowery language and phrases for you."

Peter began to hear the change in her voice. It was becoming bitter. A warning for him not to tread too far on dangerous water. He forced himself to continue on his current path. He began again using his soft voice, knowing it would sooth her, "Charlotte, you miss ruling alone, do you not? You wish time to reverse so you can continue on alone."

Charlotte stared at him through widened eyes, "Peter, I never meant to seem so. If that were true, we wouldn't have had Myla. And the Council would try to coax me into marrying some other selfish noble who is only concerned about himself and..."

Peter put a finger to her lips, stilling her. "I understand, Charlotte. You need not wear out your breath telling me more. I simply wanted to know why you were upset. I'm concerned about you, love."

Charlotte smiled, "I know you are, Peter. But I'm just tired of not doing my part with ruling."

"Well, now that Myla is turning a year perhaps you can resume ruling by my side once again."

Charlotte's eyes flooded with happiness, "Truly?"

Peter smiled and kissed her forehead, "Truly."

A shriek of terror split the air, startling everyone in the Hall. The minstrels stopped mid-song in confusion. Peter felt Charlotte stiffen under his touch. Something was wrong. The next shriek answered his prediction and filled him with horror.

"The princess has been kidnapped!"

Chapter 3

Fear surged through Peter's whole body. His mind filled with horrid images of his daughter being hauled into the unknown world. Charlotte had gone rigid beside him. Her frame the very image of fear and horror.

Alice came darting from the hallway. Tears streaked her face as she collapsed into Rowan's waiting form nearby. "They took her!" she sobbed. "They took her!"

Charlotte moved towards her friend and laid a hand on Alice's back. "Alice, what happened? Please, speak to me." Peter made his way to stand by Charlotte as Alice wailed, "They took Princess Myla! But they also stole Gavin and Faye! They stole them from right under my watch! They took them all!" Alice fell back into Rowan's arms, sobbing uncontrollably. Rowan cast a worried look at Peter.

Peter, still digesting the happening, managed to blurt out, "Who? Who took the children? I must know, Alice, you must tell me."

Alice shook her head, sniffling, "I don't know. I was following the children down the castle passageway but it was too dark in the hallway to see them properly. All I saw were shadows and the screams of Faye and Myla. One man was holding a dagger to Gavin's throat and growling, "Shut up, boy!"

Peter exchanged a glance with Rowan. Charlotte was trying to sooth Alice, but Peter knew her words were forced. Charlotte's body was tense and full of electric anxiety. Many of the guests had stopped their chatting and started over to see what the fuss was about. Peter took charge, not wanting to wait any longer. The more time he wasted, the more time the culprits had of getting away. "Charlotte," Peter said, "take Alice up to your solar and stay with her. I will handle the matter further with Rowan."

Charlotte looked about to protest against the plan, but after Peter gave her a warning glance, she nodded her consent. Charlotte drew Alice away from Rowan and steered her away from the gathering crowd. After the women had left, Peter turned to Rowan and ordered, "Tell these guests the celebration is over. Have them leave at once. I can't concern myself with them while my daughter's life is at stake."

"Yes, my king," Rowan spun around and began to quiet the guests and give them Peter's announcement.

Peter turned his mind to the next task. "Sir Richard! Sir Henry! Come quickly!" The knights came surging towards him, holding on to their sword hilts as they ran. "Myla has been…"

Sir Richard held up his hand, "We know, Your Highness. What do you want us to do? We are at your service."

"Send out a search party made up of knights to search for my daughter. Each one of you lead one party. Divide the lands into sections and don't leave any stone unturned. This must be done at once. Go now!"

With a swift bow, the knights were gone. Peter let out an anxious breath. Numerous thoughts were filling his mind. None of them were good. He needed to think of more he could do. He would never forgive himself if Myla was lost to him forever. He also believed Charlotte wouldn't be very forgiving either if he told her that their child was gone forever. He paced around the Great Hall. The Hall had emptied out, leaving only a couple of lords: Lord Edmund and Lord Geoffrey. When Peter had stopped pacing, the nobles approached him and made formal bows.

"With Your Majesty's permission, I will speak," Lord Edmund said.

"You may," Peter answered.

"We want to alert Your Highness that Lord Geoffrey and myself will be keeping a look out for Princess Myla."

"With Your Majesty's permission," Lord Geoffrey put in, "we will each send out knights of our own to seek out the present villains."

Peter nodded, a slight relief flowing into him. He was glad he had the older lords' council for this time. He could always rely on them. "Please do all you can. I need every man with noble blood in his veins to do his part."

"We will proceed, then," Lord Edmund replied. "We assure you, my king, nothing will go unnoticed on our watch."

"Then make haste and follow through with your plans," Peter ordered. "I want to make sure my daughter is back."

"As Your Majesty wishes," Lord Edmund said, bowing and backing away with Lord Geoffrey. Lord Edmund stopped. "My king?" he asked.

"Yes?"

"While we search for Princess Myla, you have another job to follow through with."

"Oh?" Peter asked, searching his scattered mind for anything else he could do. Picking up nothing he inquired, "What would that be, my lords?"

"Your queen," Lord Geoffrey replied.

"Queen Charlotte?" Peter asked in confusion.

"Yes, King Peter," Lord Edmund said, "She is fretting over her lost child, no doubt. She needs comforting."

Lord Edmund was right. The last thing he remembered doing was sending her away. How could he have forgotten her so soon? Was his mind that blurred? "Yes," Peter said, "I take it she is nervous. I should go to her."

"Yes, you must," Lord Edmund replied. "It's best if you stay with her. Comfort her, for she shall need it."

When the lords had made their farewell, Peter had a few words with Rowan, instructing him to comfort Alice. After that, Peter started up the stairs to Charlotte's solar. But, as he had seen many times, Charlotte's temper was unpredictable. No noble knew her true demeanor like he did. She wasn't one to be comforted easily. Not if there was still more to do about a matter. Peter knew she meant well when she insisted on helping, but he needed to keep her safe. He would break his last promise to King Philip if he let anything happen to her. The question nagging at his mind remained unanswered. Would Charlotte reject his comfort or receive it?

Chapter 4

Charlotte paced around her solar in sheer anxiety as she struggled to comprehend what had happened this evening. Kidnapped. Her daughter had been kidnapped. There was no mistaking that fact. Her head swam with terror for her missing child. Myla must be terrified and crying for her mother, wondering where the culprits were taking her.

Charlotte heard footsteps in the hall and turned to see Peter walking in. His face was ashen and his normally cheerful eyes were clouded with anxiety. Charlotte hurried to his side. "Is anything being done?"

Peter seemed to notice her worried state and calmed himself down, talking in a calm voice, "Charlotte, don't fret so. Before I did anything more I wanted to see if you were well."

"I'm fine!" Charlotte snapped. "What I want to know is if you've done anything."

Peter switched to a different topic, much to Charlotte's disgust. "Where is Alice? I sent you both up here."

"She's with Rowan in their room. Now, answer me, Peter. Have you done anything?"

"I told you I wanted to see if you were all right first," Peter replied. He kept looking at her in worriment. "By your attitude, you're stressed. You need to calm down."

"I will once you do something about this," Charlotte retorted.

"I sent my best knights out on a search party. The culprits won't get far. My knights know this land better than anyone."

"And what will you do if they can't find them?" Charlotte shot back.

Peter pulled her into his arms, "Charlotte, please don't dwell on 'what ifs'."

She jerked away and frowned, "Our child is missing. Not just ours, but Alice and Rowan's as well. I can't just wait to see what happens. I need to know every alternative."

Peter sighed, "If they find nothing then I'm going myself with another group. We won't return until Myla is found."

"Then I'm going with you."

Peter's eyes turned frozen, "No Charlotte, it's too dangerous. I will do this alone with the men I trust."

Charlotte backed farther away from him, outraged at what she had just heard. "Are you saying you don't trust me? You want me to stay here? Myla, our child, is out there alone and you want me to stay behind? Peter, I've never heard the like! I'm going!"

Peter pinched the bridge of his nose, a sign that his patience was wearing thin. "Charlotte...please just listen to me for once."

"What do you mean listen to you for once?" Charlotte berated. "I've listened to you many times. You make it sound like I never listen to you."

"Charlotte, this is different..."

"No! It's not different!" She stormed around the solar, "Myla is in trouble! My girl is gone! I'm going!"

Peter met her gaze. His eyes were stone cold. Charlotte felt a tremor of fear roll down her spine. She'd never seen him this angry before. "No, you're not."

"Why?" she challenged.

Peter stalked towards her and Charlotte felt herself become defensive. Her stone walls rose over her heart. If he stood in her way from helping their daughter then so be it. He made himself her enemy. He stood in front of her, his blue eyes piercing her.

"Why?" she challenged, making sure he had heard her.

He parted his mouth as if to say something then closed it. Instead, Peter pulled her into his arms and hugged her to himself in a tight embrace. "I love you," he whispered against her hair.

Charlotte refused to be swayed. "You didn't answer my question."

"I did, Charlotte. That's my answer. I love you. That's why I don't want you to go. I can't bear to lose you too."

Charlotte struggled to get loose, but Peter's grip never lessened. "Charlotte, you must listen to me. You must understand this. I can't lose you. I've almost lost you once, I'm not taking that chance again." He released her just enough to look into her eyes, "Do you understand?"

"But..." she began, "I want to help."

"Not this time, my love," Peter stroked her face. "I have to protect you as well."

"I can protect myself," Charlotte retorted.

Peter leaned his head against her forehead, "That's what I fear most. Your confidence could lead you into trouble. I don't want that."

"But..."

Peter held up his hand. "No Charlotte, please listen to my reasoning. I don't want to lose you. I couldn't bear that loss. You're too precious. Myla needs a mother to look after her when we return. How could I do that if you suddenly disappeared or worse?"

Charlotte looked into his eyes. He really was worried about her. She hadn't had many people worry about her, much less care about what she did. But Peter cared.

She fixed her eyes on the floor. She couldn't fight with him. It wouldn't get her anywhere. Instead she would try a different tactic that she hated. But Myla's life was in her hands. She must do this for her beloved daughter. She began to take on a submissive, defeated posture. "All right, Peter. I will let you handle this further."

Peter breathed a sigh of relief, "Thank you, Charlotte."

Charlotte smiled on the inside. He had taken her bait.

Peter stood up straight. "Now, you rest, my beloved. I have to see to a few details about my trip if I must leave."

"Do you really believe you will have to leave?" Charlotte asked, still playing her submissive game.

Peter smiled at her gently, "We shall see. But don't go worrying over such matters. I have it all under control."

Charlotte nodded and cast her eyes to the floor. A hand lifted her chin and Peter's frown met her gaze. He seemed to suspect something. Perhaps she had overdone her act. He could very well be suspicious. She never acted like this. But, instead of asking why she was so submissive, he shrugged as if it was nothing.

Peter leaned close to her again. "Charlotte, I promise I will bring Myla home. No matter what the cost."

Charlotte only nodded. Peter drew her away and looked at her through teary eyes. He wrapped an arm around her waist, grazed his fingers over her hair and down her cheek, and kissed her gently. "I will see you later tonight. If the knights return empty-handed, I will leave early tomorrow morning."

She nodded and watched as he walked out. After Peter left, Charlotte made it her responsibility to start packing for her trip. If Peter was to leave in the morning, she would leave near midnight while everyone was asleep. She glanced at Luna and Ferox curled up near the hearth. Peter thought she wouldn't be protected. Well she would be. Luna had been her protector far longer than he had. With Luna by her side, along with Ferox, Charlotte could guarantee nothing would happen to her. As she packed, Charlotte perked up at the sound of thunder. The signal of an upcoming storm.

———————

Simon leaned against King Peter's stone wall. Sir Richard and Sir Henry stood against the opposite side. Each man was waiting for the king to return from his errand to the queen. Because of the tragic news Simon and the others had to report, the wait was dreaded. They had found no sign of the culprits in Peter's kingdom. The kidnappers had vanished without a trace. Simon was still wondering how they would manage to break the news to Peter. How in the world were you supposed to tell a father that his child is gone? The notion seemed impossible.

Footsteps echoed in the hallway, making the knights look toward the door. A brown-haired youth of twenty-one made his entrance, the royal emblem emblazoned on his sword hilt and sheath. Simon bowed with the other knights and waited for his order to rise.

"You may stand, my noble knights," Peter said.

Simon obeyed along with the others.

"Now," the king began, "tell me, what news do you bring?"

Simon gulped. The knights exchanged uncertain glances. Who would dare tell Peter the news?

Finally, Sir Richard broke the silence. His reply seemed to echo haughtily across the Great Hall. "I'm afraid we have unfortunate news, Your Highness," he said.

Simon watched as Peter's eyes clouded with misery. The young king was obviously trying to control his disappointment. It wasn't every day that you found out your child was missing.

"We were unable to track down the kidnappers," Sir Henry continued for Sir Richard. "In this darkness it was impossible to find tracks."

A crackle of thunder sounded from outside. Rain started to pour from the heavens, creating an even more dismal atmosphere.

Simon observed Peter. The young man's face was the perfect picture of disappointment, anger, and misery combined. Simon forced his gaze away, unable to look upon the king's broken state any longer.

"Please, my king, forgive us," Sir Richard said. "I assure you that we will continue our search tomorrow."

"Rowan!" Peter shouted.

Simon flinched as Peter's fury cracked around the room, similar to that of the thunder outside.

Rowan appeared by the doorway, "Yes, Your Highness?"

Peter jerked his head for the steward to join them. "Come, we must make a plan to search for my daughter and your children tomorrow."

"Of course, my king."

When Rowan was beside Simon, Peter began. "Sir Richard, when do you suggest is the best time for departure?"

"The sun rises early in the morning, Your Highness," the knight answered. "The earlier you leave, the better."

"Very well," Peter said. "I expect you, Sir Richard, to stay here. I want you to guard and patrol Aurum until I return."

"I will do so with honor, my king," Sir Richard replied, bowing.

Peter turned to Rowan and Simon, "You two are coming along."

"Of course, my king," Simon said.

Rowan nodded next to him.

To all of them, Peter said, "Queen Charlotte will be ruling until I return. Those who stay are to give her their full attention and respect. She is just as capable of ruling Aurum as I am. Rowan, I will put the bailiff in your place until we return.

At the first light of dawn, meet me down by the stables. Bring only necessary supplies, we don't want to give our horses a burden. Do I make my plan clear?"

"Yes, my king," they chorused together.

"Good," Peter replied. "Now, rest and prepare yourselves, for we have a long journey ahead of us."

Lightening shot through the dark night sky as Charlotte strapped the saddle to Luna's back. Thunder rumbled from far off and rain poured down from the weeping clouds. Charlotte let out a groan. It would be more difficult for Luna and Ferox to fly in this weather. Presently Ferox was pacing back and forth, letting out growls whenever lightening lit up the sky.

Charlotte finished strapping the saddle and leather bag to Luna and approached the other black griffin. She ran her fingers through Ferox's thick fur to comfort the younger griffin. Ferox was still inexperienced but hopefully this trip would change the beast.

"Where do you think you're going?" a voice asked, making Charlotte whirl around.

Alice was standing in the doorway of the stable. A lightening bolt chose that moment to strike, illuminating her friend's features. Alice's hands were on her hips, her eyes were swollen and moist from crying but demanding to know what Charlotte was doing out in the stables at midnight.

Luna was growling under her breath. Charlotte settled the griffin and approached Alice. "I'm going after my daughter," she announced, "and your children as well."

Alice nodded, "I see." Then she frowned and inquired, "With the king's permission?"

Charlotte was baffled. Would Peter really give her permission to go out alone in the middle of the night in a thunderstorm? Of course not! He would be furious with the very idea! He would demand that she wait for him to come along. "No," was all Charlotte said.

"Charlotte!" Alice gasped. "You really intend to go out alone? There are numerous dangers! Your husband would forbid it!"

"Which is why I have no intention of letting Peter know," Charlotte replied. "He's asleep for the time being and when he wakes, I will be miles away. He won't be able to do anything about it."

"What if something happens to you?" Alice asked, walking closer.

"I'm willing to take that risk. If Myla's life is in danger and Peter doesn't want to act straight away, then it's up to me."

"This is a foolhardy decision Charlotte!" Alice exclaimed. "This isn't something you've done before. You don't know what to expect!"

"I don't care!" Charlotte shot back. "Nothing is standing in my way from helping my daughter! If anyone does, they make themselves my enemy!"

Alice stepped away from her friend's infuriated form. She, above everyone else knew how dangerous Charlotte could become when crossed. No one would want to be responsible for standing in the queen's way. She knew she had no power to stop her friend from carrying out her plan. But she could do something to improve it.

"Fine," Alice replied, "if you wish to go along with this foolish decision of yours go on."

Charlotte's expression was one of surprise. "You...you mean you're allowing me to pass that easily?" she asked. "I thought you would try and give me more of a hassle."

Alice held up her finger, not caring how disrespectful such an act was. Charlotte was her friend and she knew the queen wouldn't mind her doing so. "On one condition."

"And what would that be?" Charlotte inquired.

"That you allow me to come with you."

"No," Charlotte answered firmly. "Rowan would be furious. Not just with me but with you. He cares about you a lot and I don't want to be responsible for making him angry."

"I said the same thing to you about the king," Alice retorted. "And you insisted upon going against his wishes. You will need help. What if you get sick? I'll be the person to nurse you back to life. At least for your health's and my children's sake let me come."

Alice smiled to herself when Charlotte began to pace the stables. She knew she had left her defenseless. Growing up with the young queen, Alice knew how to convince Charlotte. At least in some ways.

Charlotte sighed, "You may come. But," she turned toward Alice, her green eyes flashing against the dark atmosphere, "you will travel under my conditions. You will ride on a griffin and carry weapons, a sword and dagger."

"Very well," Alice agreed. "And I will also supply the medicine. Who knows when we might need it."

Charlotte nodded. "But only a little. You can find more plants on the trail."

"Of course," Alice replied.

As she watched Charlotte begin to saddle Ferox for the trip, questions began to form in her mind. Charlotte was skilled on finding people and planning for battles. But would she be enough? At least with the men they would have had more protection. But they were alone. Two women going out into the unknown with only one skilled in swordsmanship.

Chapter 5

Peter woke up to the pinkish light of dawn. The outside world was full of the birds' cheerful morning songs. It was hard to believe that last night Myla had been kidnapped. At the thought of his missing daughter, Peter was wide awake. If light was filtering into his room that meant dawn was upon them. Gingerly, he felt for Charlotte's back where she had fallen asleep last night. The sheets were cold where her warm body had lain. Alarmed, he sat up and looked around. Charlotte was gone.

Flinging himself out of bed and scrambling into his morning robe, Peter shoved aside the tapestry dividing the room. Charlotte wasn't in her usual spot by the hearth.

A servant entered and set a bowl of fruit down on the table.

"Man, have you seen the queen?" Peter demanded, walking up to the table.

"No, Your Excellence," the servant replied. "I would think that she would be with you."

This couldn't be happening. "Well, she isn't," Peter retorted.

"Forgive me for not being of any help, Your Majesty," the servant apologized. "Perhaps her maids shall know."

"Yes, perhaps," Peter murmured. But deep down, he was beginning to think they wouldn't. "You are dismissed. Send my wife's two favorite handmaids into the Great Hall, I would like to question them."

"Yes, my king," the servant answered. Bowing, he backed out of the room.

The maids entered the Hall shortly after he had. Mary and Amity were Charlotte's two favorite maids and seemed to know more about Charlotte than the rest of her ladies. If something happened to Charlotte they were Peter's only hope of knowing.

"Your Highness and exalted ruler of Aurum," Mary said, bowing, "you sent for us. What is it you wish?"

"Yes, Your Excellence," Amity said, bowing next to Mary. "We await Your Highness' orders."

"Have you seen Queen Charlotte?" Peter demanded. "She wasn't at breakfast."

Mary and Amity exchanged glances. "We have not, my king. I am sorry."

"That is all I needed to know," Peter said. Giving a dismissive wave to the maids, he added, "You may go."

Shortly after the maids left, Rowan came bursting in. "Forgive me, Your Majesty, but I have been looking for you everywhere! I have terrible news!"

"I know," Peter replied. He had a feeling he knew what was coming. He could sense it in the air.

Rowan cocked his head, "You know?"

"Does it have anything to do with my missing queen?" Peter inquired, getting down from his throne and approaching his steward.

Rowan's eyes widened, "Queen Charlotte is missing as well?"

"What do you mean 'as well'?" Peter asked.

"Alice is gone!" Rowan exclaimed. "She disappeared! I can't find her anywhere!" Rowan's temper began to turn hotter. "First my children and now my wife! Those men will pay for this!"

Peter put a hand on Rowan's shoulder, "Be still, Rowan, for it is not what you think."

"What do you mean?" Rowan asked. "The kidnappers weren't satisfied with just the children. They decided they may as well take our women too." Rowan began to grow angry again. "I swear if they do any harm to Alice I'll..."

"The kidnappers did not take your wife or the queen," Peter interrupted before Rowan could get into the details.

"Then who did, my king?" Rowan's question held that of a slight challenge.

"No one kidnapped them. They went off on their own," Peter informed. "At least Charlotte did. She went against my wishes and decided to hunt down the culprits herself. Your wife probably was trying to stop our queen from doing so and ended up going with her. Do not ask me why your wife also went. That is for you to ask her."

Rowan stared at Peter for a long time without speaking. Finally, his voice seemed to find him. In a whisper he asked, "My king, what shall we do?"

"We will find them," Peter reassured. "I am confident that Charlotte would go the same way I intended to go. I'm certain we shall run into them in our travels. When we do, we must decide whether to send them back or to let them come along."

Rowan nodded in agreement.

"Now, it is already past dawn and our fellow countrymen are waiting by the stables. Ready yourself and make haste for if we wish to catch up with them we must hurry. Once my wife decides to follow through with something she rarely ever stops."

Charlotte covered her mouth as another cough came up her throat. The cool dawn breeze blew in her face as she rode atop of Luna. Alice, hearing her cough, flew up alongside her with Ferox. "Charlotte, you have been coughing for quite awhile. We should land and I should give you some medicine."

Charlotte shook her head, "I'm fine, Alice." She knew better than to land in the middle of nowhere. If they didn't land in a town or at least a village, they would have the disadvantage of meeting up with Peter, or worse, a band of thieves.

"I insist," Alice went on, "how are you going to help your daughter if you grow weaker?"

At this point, Charlotte had to admit that Alice was correct. If she pushed herself too far she would be of little use to Myla when the time came. She sighed, "Very well, Alice, but just for a short time. I don't want to take chances."

Alice looked at her oddly then shrugged off her concern. Charlotte hadn't told Alice about the dangers and it was better that way. She didn't want to worry her friend over the matter. However, when they landed, Charlotte made sure they were in an open field cleared of all surrounding trees.

Alice leapt off of Ferox's back and began to sort out her medicine supply. Alice shooed Charlotte off when she tried to help. "Go sit and rest. This shouldn't take long but you don't get any rest when you're riding."

Charlotte was about to protest when Alice shot her a glare. Shrugging, Charlotte slid to the ground next to Luna.

Leaning against her griffin's soft fur, Charlotte realized how tired she was. Up in the air she couldn't fall asleep without risking her neck trying to stay on the saddle. She closed her eyes and let sleep overtake her.

———————

"Charlotte?"

Charlotte's eyes flew open at the sound of Alice's uncertain voice. Fear was apparent in Alice's call. Something was wrong. Getting up, Charlotte walked over to where Alice cowered near Ferox. Both black griffins were growling at something ahead of them. Their ears lay flat against their heads and the fur on their backs stood on end. Only then did Charlotte realize there was silence all around them. Not a bird called. Something had startled them.

Charlotte peered into the distance where the griffins and Alice were looking. Shadows moved towards them. Charlotte didn't have to think twice on who they were. They were thieves and they had every intention of robbing them.

Alice tugged at Charlotte's sleeve and pleaded, "Charlotte, let's go. We can fly to somewhere else. Please."

Charlotte's gaze floated to the weapons the thieves carried. Three of the men carried crossbows. "We can't."

"Why not?" Alice asked in desperation.

"Because they can shoot us down," Charlotte answered. "They'll end up hurting us more if we try to fly away. Our best bet is to stand firm and face them head on." Charlotte began to count them. There were six in all. They were hopelessly outnumbered.

"But…"

"Alice, listen to me," Charlotte interrupted. "You are to remain behind me at all times. Keep your dagger at hand and be ready to kill if necessary."

Alice's eyes widened in fright, "Kill if necessary?"

"That's right," Charlotte replied. "No nonsense. If they approach you, you stab them. Understood?"

Alice shivered, "Very well. You know what's best."

Charlotte nodded, "I'll try to ward off most of them but it's best to be prepared. There are six of them and only two of us plus the griffins. We stand a chance, if you cooperate."

The thieves had come into a close enough proximity to make Charlotte stop talking. She shot one more warning glare at Alice before facing the group of men. They were rugged and their grim faces meant business. Despite Charlotte's hope, not one thief seemed fazed by the spitting griffins behind Charlotte.

One man, who was obviously the leader, stepped forward, "All right, lasses, what do you have on you?"

"Nothing you want," Charlotte answered simply, making sure her voice sounded firm.

"Now, now, lass, you surely have something we want. Jewels or gold?" The leader was approaching quickly.

"We have none," Charlotte answered. Her stone walls started to enclose her heart. No one would get past her. She would make certain of that. These men were her enemies.

"Well," the leader said, "you certainly have something else we want. Me in particular." The man was staring at Charlotte with a dangerous glint in his eyes. One of his bolder followers was advancing and had eyes only for Alice. Alice was shaking and staring at the thief in fright.

Charlotte made a move towards the advancing thief but kept her eyes on the leader. "You aren't harming her or me."

The leader only laughed along with the rest. "Oh yes, I have heard that story before. But, without any male bodyguards, you lasses are in a sorry state."

Charlotte's hand was innocently reaching for her concealed dagger. Even when she had her sword by her side, she preferred to take her enemy by surprise with her dagger. The more surprise she gave her attacker, the more advantage she had.

The leader was too intent on watching her face that he didn't seem to notice her simple but deadly movement. Charlotte cast a glance at the other thief eyeing Alice.

Now.

In one swift movement, the dagger was in her hand and then flying through the air straight into the chest of Alice's pursuer. The dagger remained implanted in the man's skin as he let out a cry of shock, collapsing on top of the knife, dead.

Charlotte's gaze had never left the leader's. Instead, her sharp gaze hardened into a threatening manner as she hissed, "That is a warning."

At the sight of their owner making a kill, Luna and Ferox were tearing at the ground impatient to follow her example. Their claws craved the soft flesh of their enemy. But, they remained still, waiting for Charlotte's signal to attack. Out of the corner of her eye, Charlotte saw thieves begin to fan out and surround her, Alice, and the griffins. Charlotte waited.

Alice was whimpering and on the verge of crying. Still, Charlotte waited until her enemy was in a complete circle around them. Then, with a slight flick of her wrist, the griffins attacked. In the first few moments, she could see only a flurry of movement and the screams of terror from the bandits.

As the scene cleared, Charlotte picked out the two griffins, snarling and seething, attacking two of the men. Even when one of the men joined the broil to help his comrades, Charlotte was hopelessly outnumbered. The leader and another man ignored the pleas for help and started towards Charlotte.

Careful not to trip over the dead body by her side, Charlotte backed away and drew her sword. Alice was backing away as well and staring at the ruffians wide-eyed. Charlotte studied her opponent, searching for his motive or weakness. The leader's eyes gleamed at Charlotte. Obviously he was thinking of more than just stealing money from her. From her speech she knew he could tell she came from a wealthy background. With this in mind, he could easily hold her and Alice for ransom. He had no intention of killing her with money involved, only disarming her. In this way, Charlotte held the advantage.

The leader lashed out at Charlotte's legs, trying to trip her. Charlotte jumped to avoid the injury and, before her opponent could react, landed and swung the flat of her blade around to hit him in the neck. The man grimaced in pain and staggered backwards. Before she could finish him off, his follower landed a swift blow to her sword arm, making Charlotte grunt. She fumbled to stop another heavy blow as it came crashing down. By the time Charlotte had regained her footing, the leader had recovered and was advancing towards her. His friend was walking to where Alice stood. In her desperation, Alice drew her dagger. The man only smirked and continued towards her.

Before Charlotte could think, an arrow whistled through the air. The sound ended as it hit the leader near

Charlotte, sinking into his chest. The man collapsed at Charlotte's feet in an unmoving heap. Without his leader's guidance, the other thief seemed lost. Without any hesitation and without checking where the arrow had come from, Charlotte jabbed her sword into the man's flesh, killing him.

Charlotte looked around. Luna and Ferox had done their job and were sitting by their kills proudly. The sound of horses' hooves upon the dirt path brought Charlotte's gaze upward. Across from her gory surroundings, a group of knights were riding towards them. That answered the question as to where the arrow had come from. Only when the horses drew nearer did Charlotte realize who was astride them. She let out a groan when she saw the royal emblem of the golden griffin on blood red fabric.

―――――――――

Peter swung down from his courser even before his horse had stopped galloping. Tossing his crossbow to Simon, he hurried over to where Charlotte stood amongst the dead. He followed her gaze as she watched Alice collapse into Rowan's arms, trembling and weeping. Finally, she seemed to drag her eyes to him, emblazoning her green gaze into his soul. Peter stopped a good distance away and opened his arms, hoping she would run to him. He expected too much. Her feet remained planted in place. Peter let out a sigh and walked over to her. Why must she be this way? In some moments, he wished she would be more like Alice in her affections toward him. But, Charlotte would never be like that. Her harsh childhood had made its mark and forever he would have to battle for her love.

Charlotte's arms were crossed and her glare was searing into his eyes. She was angry. And she was not a force to be reckoned with when she was infuriated. He decided it was best to try and make peace with her. Not to express his anger and hurt back at her for disobeying him. He would start off gently.

He ran a hand over her cheek. She flinched. He spoke softly, "This is the reason I wanted you to stay at the castle. I wanted you to be safe."

"I was fine," Charlotte spat. She shoved his hand away. Evidently she wasn't going to give in without a fight. "And maybe I would also be fine if you agreed to go with me in the beginning," she snarled.

Peter frowned, "Charlotte, it wouldn't have made much of a difference. It makes more sense to leave at dawn when you can see."

"I only wanted to help find my daughter!" she shouted.

"And so did I," Peter replied. His calmness was crumbling. She was making this more difficult than necessary. "Now, neither of us are doing so. Instead, we're standing over dead bodies wasting time."

"You're one to talk of wasting time!" she snapped. "You're the one who..."

"Enough!" Peter interrupted, raising his voice. "I didn't want to do this but you leave me no choice. I'm sending you home."

"What?" Charlotte exclaimed in rage. "Why?" she demanded.

Peter became aware of the others watching them. He hated the feeling of having his subjects watch their monarchs fight. He forced himself to continue. "The reason is because you disobeyed my wishes. You went behind my back and did deliberately what I told you not to do. Charlotte, you must understand that I set certain boundaries to protect you."

Charlotte was still glaring at him. But, in her gaze he saw a flash of unease come and go.

He went on, "In disobeying me you not only put yourself but also Alice in danger. I'm disappointed in you."

Charlotte was close to tears now. Whether they were tears of frustration or sadness, Peter did not know. He only wished they would be of sadness. That way he would have an excuse to pull her into his arms after nearly losing her to thieves. Charlotte raised a hand as if to lash out. Peter braced himself, but the blow never came. Instead, she covered her mouth and coughed. The sound of the terrible, harsh, rough coughs disturbed Peter. All the more reason to send her back. "See now, you're sick. If you let me go on then you can..."

"I'm fine," she snapped. "I'm coming with you and you can't stop me."

"Charlotte, I don't want to fight with you over this..."

35

"Good, then it's settled. Alice and I are coming with you," Charlotte interrupted.

"It is not settled at all," Peter replied. "I'm not dragging you and Alice into danger."

"I'll fight you if I have to." Charlotte's hiss echoed across the land. "Nothing stands in my way of helping Myla." Peter knew she meant every word.

"My king."

Peter turned as Rowan approached them. "Yes, Rowan?"

"Alice insists on coming along," his steward began, "she says she can help cure us if one of us gets sick." Rowan glanced at Charlotte. "I think you must let the queen come. It's not very suiting to have Alice travel without another woman in the company of men."

Peter ran a hand over his face and looked at his wife. Her eyes were hard and determined, as was her stance. He was still a long way from convincing her to return to their castle. "Very well," he sighed. "I will send a message to the fortress saying Lord Edmund is in charge of our lands until we return."

Charlotte's eyes lit up. Her sudden victory seemed to excite her.

"But," Peter added, holding up a finger, "you will no longer disobey me. On this trip you will follow my orders, not your own. Is that clear?"

"Fine," Charlotte replied. She brushed past him in a defiant manner. "As long as I can come."

In relief, Peter walked over to Simon. "Do you mind helping Rowan and the knights bury the dead. I don't want to leave such a mess in the road."

"Of course, my king." Simon slid to the ground and began to follow through with his orders.

Peter glanced at Charlotte. Alice was giving her something to chew. As far as Peter could see, whatever Charlotte was eating tasted foul. But, she seemed to be getting over her angry streak, which was a relief. Peter would hate to be on Charlotte's bad side for their journey. He needed her and he was almost certain she would need him. Because, however hard the other dangers had been for them, this new threat promised to be much more challenging.

Chapter 6

Peter's mount plodded along in front of the group. With a clear road ahead he risked a look back at the rest of his company. In the back were three other knights from his garrison each on the look out for more danger. Rowan came next in the line with Alice on the back of his saddle, still sniffling softly. Simon rode the closest to him and would dart his eyes around at the slightest noise. Peter turned his attention back to the front, guiding his horse over loose rocks in the old, Roman road. Once clear of the gravel, he looked up. Luna and Ferox were soaring above him, with Charlotte riding on Luna's back. Ever since their argument a couple of hours ago, Charlotte had remained distant from him. She had not so much as made eye contact with him. When they had taken to the trail again, she had ignored his hand for a ride on his courser and instead had mounted Luna and flown off.

Sighing, Peter turned his gaze back to the road. He would have to approach her soon. He needed to reassure himself that she wasn't hurt. The only thing holding him back was that he never knew what to expect from her.

A small serf village came into view down in the valley ahead of him. Peter raised a hand to stop the group and motioned Rowan forward. His steward trotted his horse up beside Peter's, "My king?"

Peter pointed to the serf village, "I want to stop in there and ask around. You couldn't possibly escape this village without notice. If we wish to find the culprits, we'll start by asking questions to the villagers. They are most likely to know."

"Of course, Your Majesty," Rowan replied. He patted Alice's white-knuckled hand in reassurance. "We are going to stop and ask these villagers some questions, my dear. Perhaps we'll find out where Gavin and Faye are," he whispered.

Peter looked up once again. Luna and Ferox were circling the group. With a wave, he caught Charlotte's eye and pointed to the village. He saw her nod briefly and watched as she flew away towards the thatched cottages. Kicking his stallion, Peter waved the company forward.

Peter guided his courser to a large oak tree outside the town's old, stone wall. Charlotte landed beside the knight's horses, startling the poor animals into a panicked frenzy. Peter watched as she slipped from Luna's back and stalked over to him. She crossed her arms and looked at him with expectancy. Peter had the rising feeling that it was meant as a challenge. How in all the world did she make such simple gestures or eye contact stronger than it really was? Peter waited until the rest of the knights along with Simon, Rowan and Alice were dismounted until he spoke. "We are here because I feel the urge to ask the villagers if they have seen anything suspicious. Now, you each have roles to play in this and I expect the best out of all of you. Without Myla, Aurum's future is uncertain. If our kingdom is to survive, you must all do your best. A dagger is pointed right at Aurum's heart. If she is to survive, we must knock the blade away and capture the bandits. And," Peter added, meeting Rowan's concerned gaze, "wherever Myla is, your children are also. If we find her, we'll find them."

A murmur of approval echoed through the group.

Peter continued, "Now, Simon I want you along with Sir Adam to ask and scope out the land to the west. I will take the east along with Sir William and Sir Gilbert." Peter turned to Rowan. "Rowan, I want you to stay here with Alice and Charlotte. I believe the women have had enough excitement for one day."

Peter caught Charlotte's searing glare. He knew she was trying her best not to snap at him in front of the whole company. But, behind the anger, swam tears in her lovely eyes. He continued, "We will all meet back here in a couple of hours whether we're successful or not. If we are, then we will follow the bandits' trail. If we're not..." Peter trailed off. He didn't want to think of that possibility. He forced himself to voice it anyway. "If we aren't, then we will have to keep looking; searching for clues in any possible place."

Charlotte wandered down the hill to a weathered, stone wall. After Peter had left with the other knights for the search she decided she would give Alice and Rowan some alone time. After the morning's events, the least Charlotte could do for her friend was give her some space with her husband. It was also best for her as well. When Rowan had carried Alice over to the tree and laid her head on his shoulder, Charlotte knew she needed to leave. Whenever Rowan and Alice showed their deep affection for each other in front of her, she felt a strange surge of longing crash over her. She and Peter never really displayed their love quite so well in public. Even in private Charlotte felt nervous or reserved towards him. Never having a mother or governess to guide her, she didn't know how to play her role as Peter's wife. As a mother it was easier, for she had been around children in her younger age in the serf village. But as a wife...

She sighed and plopped her arms on the stone wall that enclosed a grassy field. But, Peter was exceptionally patient with her more than she'd expected. He never pushed her for affection. And whenever he wanted to express his love to her it was in a gentle and caring way. But, he rarely did it. When she saw Alice and Rowan's affectionate embraces, she felt a yearning deep down that made her wish Peter would do the same. Tears welled up in her eyes and she wiped at them viciously. No, it would never be that way with them. Not at the moment anyway. She was still mad at him for thinking of her as irresponsible and disobedient. Was she not the one who killed the bandits? Was she not the one who thought of her daughter above all else? No, she wouldn't forgive him quite yet. Instead, she would mind what she was told but send him subtle messages that she was still upset. He needed to learn that he couldn't get away with ordering her around that easily.

———————————

Peter trudged wearily back towards Rowan and the girls in disappointment. He, along with Sir William and Sir Gilbert, had covered the whole west side of the village with nothing to show for it. Seeing that Simon and Sir Adam hadn't returned yet, gave Peter hope. His daughter was still far from his reach. His only hope was that Simon might have found something.

Rowan sat against the tree with Alice's head resting on his shoulder. Peter frowned when Charlotte didn't appear. He looked up to the sky. Would she ever do as he told her? Would she ever realize that what he did was because he loved her? Rowan noted his puzzlement and nodded towards a stone wall. Peter turned and saw Charlotte leaning against it, her dark hair blowing in the slight breeze. Rowan gave him an encouraging smile and nodded towards Charlotte again. Peter took a deep breath and started down the hill towards her. As he approached, he saw Charlotte's shoulders tense and she swung around, eyes flashing. He stopped in front of her, close enough to reach out and touch her. Before he got carried away, Peter ran a hand through his hair, to stop it from pulling Charlotte against him. He began softly as he always did when she was upset, "Charlotte, I have something to tell you."

"What?" she demanded. "Make haste and say it and then leave me alone."

Peter was startled. He hadn't expected such a sharp reply. Especially since he had kept his distance since their fight. "I only wanted to apologize for my behavior earlier. I should have listened to your point and spoken softer. Especially after what happened with the robbers." He broke off and looked at her.

Her eyebrows cocked up, as if willing him to continue.

He took her hand in his and pressed a kiss to her soft skin. "I never thought to comfort you. I'm deeply sorry, Charlotte. I acted rashly." He locked her gaze with sincere eyes and trailed a hand down her cheek.

She flinched and tensed even more.

Peter ran his hand from her cheekbone to her shoulder and began to rub it. He moved his other hand to the opposite shoulder and did the same. The tenseness began to leave. "Are you hurt? Did they hurt you?"

She only shook her head. Her shoulder's rolled back and a deep breath was released. Her eyes flickered closed then opened up to his.

"Will you forgive me, Charlotte?" he whispered. "I promise to do better in the future. Please, my love, just give me another chance."

———

Charlotte stared into Peter's honest blue gaze. Tears started to well up in her eyes. She could feel frustration and confusion mounting like the construction of a stone wall. Why did he have to make this so difficult? When he was away, she had vowed to herself to refuse any apology he had or anything he had to say. But, instead, she had said one harsh comment and he began to speak to her gently. He caressed her skin so softly and asked for her forgiveness when she was the one who should be asking for his. She was so confused. Part of her wanted to remain angry with him while the other wanted to forgive him and give him another chance. A tear fell from her eye and slid down her cheek.

Peter brushed it away. "Charlotte?" he asked in a whisper.

More tears began to fall, streaming down her cheeks in a long line. Anger was burning in her even stronger now. But not at Peter. At herself. How could she resort to crying in front of him? Only a weakling cried. What was she even crying about? Did she have any reason to shed tears?

"Charlotte, love, why are you crying?" Peter asked, concern evident in every syllable. "Is it something I said?"

Charlotte shook her head, "I don't...I don't know...I don't know why..."

Peter put a finger to her lips. Pulling her into an embrace, he said against her hair, "You're upset and confused. You don't know how to act. You don't know how to express your feelings to me."

How did he dictate so simply what she thought; what she was feeling? Leaning against him, she began to surrender to his comfort and calm herself. She inhaled and exhaled deeply, closed her eyes, and began to sway back and forth as Peter rocked her. Feeling as if a burden was lifted from her weary shoulders, she pulled away and looked up at her husband. "All right, Peter. I'll forgive you. I'll give you another chance."

Relief flooded Peter at Charlotte's answer. He leaned his forehead against hers to tell her he appreciated her words. "Thank you, Charlotte. I promise I'll do better in the future."

She bowed her head, "As will I. I really will try to be the wife you deserve to have."

Peter pulled away and tilted her chin up to look at him. "You already are what I want and I'll have you no other way. I love you for you, not who you want to be."

The sound of a horse's neigh made Charlotte turn away from him. A blue mare cantered into the field behind the stone wall. Peter watched in awe as the creature reared then started to canter around the pasture again. Slowing to a halt, the mare bent her magnificent neck and began to graze. Peter took the time to study the horse as she filled her stomach. He had never seen a horse like her. She had an exotic, deep blue coat, a star upon her head, a jet black mane and tail, and sturdy, long legs made to carry a queen. Peter didn't have to think twice about what he saw, she was a prize animal. He was about to make the comment to Charlotte when her gaze stopped him. Charlotte's eyes were shining and flooding with enchantment as she stared at the blue mare.

"She's beautiful," Charlotte whispered.

"Yes, she is," Peter replied, looking at her with love. He hadn't seen Charlotte's beautiful gaze light up since the party yesterday evening.

Charlotte looked up at him and noticed that he was staring at her. Her cheeks flamed a fetching pink and she turned her gaze back to the horse. Ever since the mare had cantered into the pasture, Peter's mind had buzzed with a sudden idea. Now, the idea would serve two purposes if Charlotte truly adored the animal. Peter couldn't see why she wouldn't. The mare was a prize; a true beauty. Just like Charlotte was.

"Do you like her, Charlotte?" he asked.

Still watching the mare, she replied, "Yes, Peter, I really do. She's fit for a..."

"Queen," Peter finished for her.

Charlotte turned to him, "Well, yes, I suppose she is. I was going to say fit to be ridden by a high born noble, but queen suits well enough."

A villager entered the pasture, clicking to the mare and shaking a bucket of oats. The mare's ears perked up at the sound and she sailed over to the man, digging her nose into the food. While the stunning creature ate, the man swung a rope over the mare's neck.

Peter saw his chance. Raising his voice, he shouted, "Here, my good man!"

The villager turned and pointed at himself, clearly uncertain if he'd been called.

"Yes, yes, come here," Peter said, waving the man over.

Charlotte looked as confused as the man did. "Peter, what on earth are you doing?" she asked, a frown creasing her brow.

"You shall see," he whispered back, as the man approached them, guiding the mare behind him.

Seeing Peter's sword and griffin emblem, the villager's eyes widened. "You called, my king?" he asked, bowing.

"Yes, yes," Peter replied. "Now, how much are you willing to charge for this fine animal? I wish to buy her and will pay any price you name."

Charlotte glanced at him with wide eyes, "Peter, what are you..."

"Well, I don't know, my king," the man stammered. "I never gave a thought to selling her. She's not easily ridden and is spooked at every sound."

Peter waved the facts off. "That makes no difference. A wild creature like this is fit for the queen herself. Many nobles would pay a number of coins for this fascinating animal."

"If you say so, Your Majesty," the villager said. He then looked at Charlotte and seemed to realize who she was. He gave another bow quickly, "Oh, my queen! Forgive me for not showing respect!"

Charlotte gestured for the man to stand up, "No need for that. You are forgiven. You needn't feel ashamed, for my husband was keeping you quite busy discussing the pricing for this lovely mare."

"Do you really adore her, Your Majesty?" the man asked.

Charlotte looked at Peter. He awaited her answer just as eagerly as the villager did. She opened her mouth to say 'yes' but it never came. She couldn't accept a gift like this after snapping at Peter. She didn't deserve it. "I...I don't think I could bare to..."

"Yes, she does," Peter interrupted. "And with that I will buy her from you. My good man, name your price."

Charlotte was taken aback at his interruption. She turned to him and whispered fiercely, "Peter, this isn't necessary. I like the mare but I don't have to have her. After this morning, I don't deserve anything this beautiful. I'll carry on riding the other horses at our castle. I've done it for so long…"

Peter put a finger to her lips, "I insist," he whispered back. "You deserve this more than you let yourself believe. She's a beautiful animal just like her soon-to-be rider. You two will get along perfectly, for your personalities are the same."

Charlotte only nodded. It was useless to argue with him. Like herself, he could be extremely stubborn when it came to something or someone he cared for.

Peter turned back to the man, "Name your price."

"Why I don't know, my king…I can't even imagine someone buying such a wild animal."

"How does twenty shillings sound?" Peter asked.

"Twenty…twenty…twenty shillings?" the man sputtered. "Twenty whole shillings?"

"Why not?" Peter answered. "That's equivalent to a good pack horse. Or should we raise the price to forty shillings? This fine mare is worth every penny I own."

Charlotte watched in amusement as the man stood before Peter speechless. Finding his words, he said, "No, no, twenty shillings is just fine."

"Good," Peter replied, nodding his approval. "Now, see that tree up on the rise?" he asked, pointing up the hill.

The villager nodded.

"Yes, bring the horse up there and I'll pay you."

The man nodded and hurried away, tugging the mare behind him.

Charlotte watched the mare dance up the hill, bucking every so often and whinnying her disapproval. After they disappeared over the rise, Charlotte turned to Peter. "Are you sure you want to buy her?"

He looked at her as if she had asked a ridiculous question. "Of course I'm sure. I saw the way you looked at the mare. You adore her and you deserve her."

Charlotte shook her head, "But why are you doing this? After the way I snapped at you, I would expect you to be angry with me."

Peter let out a small laugh. "Charlotte, I could never stay angry with you. You might have disobeyed me, but that doesn't mean I'll stay angry with you. The reason I bought her is to show you that I love you and you deserve such a prize animal."

"That's the reason you bought her?"

Peter ran a hand through his hair and cracked a smile. "There is one more reason."

Charlotte crossed her arms, "And what is that? Care to tell me?"

"The second reason is that I'm going to give you another chance to return home. The company of knights are going to return with the mare to our castle. Only Rowan, Simon, and Alice will remain. Unless, of course, if you wish to return home, then Alice will go with you."

Charlotte shook her head. No matter how many times he tried to convince her that is was unsafe, she wouldn't back down. She was in this journey to the very end. "No, Peter. My decision is final. I'm coming with you."

———————

As they walked up the hill, Peter ran over Charlotte's response in his mind. He'd known her answer before the words left her mouth. He just wanted to make sure he wasn't dragging her along. He needed to hear from her own lips that she was in this the whole way. He had tried to convince her to leave, but it had failed. Turning back was not Charlotte's thing. It never would be.

A loud, rough, cough came from next to him. Charlotte was bent forward, coughing in short, body-shaking bouts. He put his arms around her to steady her. After a few more, she straightened and continued up the hill. Peter felt a chill roll up his spine and for once, he wished he had pressured her harder to turn back.

Chapter 7

Charlotte watched as Peter dropped the silver coins into the villager's palm.

The villager cast a wary glance at the griffins not far from Charlotte before bowing to Peter. "Thank you, my king. May you live forever."

Peter shook his head, "It is I who should be thanking you for this beautiful creature. Now, before you leave, perhaps you could help us with one more matter."

The man bowed again, "Yes, of course, my king. I am your servant."

"Are you aware of the princess' recent kidnapping?" Peter asked, getting straight to the point.

The villager bowed his head, "Yes, my king. You have my utmost condolences for your tragic loss."

Charlotte perked up when she heard the man's answer. If he had heard of Myla's kidnapping perhaps he held clues as to where she could be found. Charlotte opened her mouth to demand more details when Peter held up his hand. He seemed to know she wouldn't be very subtle about the matter. Instead, she would snap and order him to tell them all he knew.

To her surprise, Peter asked calmly, "Have you seen anything peculiar that would arouse suspicion?"

Charlotte held her breath as they waited for the villager's answer. She felt Peter's hand slip into hers and squeeze tightly. Behind his calm demeanor was the same demanding spirit that she had.

"Wait a moment, my king. I think I may have something that will help you." He turned to go but then turned back, "Could you wait here until I return?"

Peter nodded, "Of course."

Simon dragged himself up the hill alongside Sir Adam. His hopes of finding any evidence that would help the king were dashed like a ship against a boulder. Any hope was being pulled under by the strong currant of despair. Now, he would have to return to the king and queen empty-handed. Having been knighted only a year ago, due to a foolish mistake in his past, Simon had all the more urge to prove himself to his monarchs. But, when a chance came to prove himself, what did he have? Nothing. Not one word of benefit on the princess' whereabouts, save the bad news that they were no closer to rescuing Peter's beloved daughter.

The remaining group came into view ahead of them. Sir William and Sir Gilbert stood underneath the tree and pointed to the trail they had just traveled on in a deep discussion with Peter. The queen stood amid the horses, stroking the muzzle of an exotic, blue mare Simon didn't recognize. Rowan and Alice still remained where they were since he and Sir Adam had left; underneath the tree with Alice resting against Rowan.

"Simon! Sir Adam!"

Simon turned to see Peter, Sir William and Sir Gilbert looking at him. Peter gestured for them to join him and the other knights. Simon nodded and trotted over to the king with Sir Adam, only to stop dead in his tracks. Peter's eyes were full with expectancy and hope. Seeing his gaze, Simon had to look away, focusing on his feet. Guilt flooded him at having to deliver the soul-crushing news to the hopeful father.

"Well," Peter prodded, "what have you found? You were gone longer than the rest."

Simon opened his mouth but the words didn't come. He closed it again, struggling to form the tragic news in his mind. How was he supposed to start?

"You found something did you not?" Peter asked, cocking his head slightly. "Speak, I beg you!"

Sir Adam seemed to find his tongue before Simon, "No, my king, we found nothing."

Simon managed to nod when Peter turned to him for a second report. "I'm sorry, my king," he said, his voice sounding hoarse. "No clues were retrieved about the princess."

Hope sank from Peter's eyes, sorrow conquering his gaze. He nodded and turned away, looking out into the village below. "Nothing," he echoed. Giving a stiff laugh, he remarked, "What did I expect? Did I really believe I could find my daughter in a day? Could I have been so naive?"

Simon hung his head and begged for the king's broken voice to be shut out. "Forgive us, my king," Simon said. "We tried our best but...but couldn't find anything that would lead us in the right direction."

"Do not lose hope, Your Majesty," Sir Gilbert said. "Remember that the villager said he might have something relevant to the situation."

"Sir Gilbert is correct, my king," Sir William added, "you may yet have something."

Peter nodded, "Yes, that is right, my knights. We may still have hope."

"Villager?" Sir Adam asked, broaching the question Simon had on his mind.

"I bought that fetching mare over there," Peter gestured, "for our queen. While I handed the money over, I asked the owner if he'd seen anything suspicious. He said he might know of something and would return shortly."

Simon nodded. Perhaps they needn't give up hope quite yet. Surely someone in this village knew about the culprits.

A sudden cough startled Simon and he watched as the queen made her way over to Peter's side. Simon saw the king's brow furrow in concern at the queen's health. The queen must have recognized Peter's concern, for she held up her hand as if telling him it was nothing of importance. Peter seemed to take her word for it and took her hands in his.

The queen's eyes looked at Simon and her green gaze narrowed. She murmured to Peter under her breath. Peter leaned forward and whispered something in the queen's ear. By the queen's broken look, Simon guessed Peter had informed her of his and Sir Adam's failed mission. As the queen fell against Peter's chest, Simon diverted his gaze and pleaded silently for the villager to bring good news. It took a tragic event to break their strong queen. Since taking the throne, nothing had rocked her firm foundation. Until now, it seemed. By her response and reactions to Peter, Simon knew this was the worst ordeal she had experienced as a queen. Nothing could compare to losing one's child.

————————

Peter looked up from where he'd been sitting with Charlotte for the past hour to the sound of running feet. The villager ran up the hill, a paper gripped in his fist. Charlotte jumped up at the sight of the man and Peter followed. This was their last hope. The man slowed to a halt, bowing over breathless in front of them. Seeing the person they had waited for, Peter's knights made their way over. Rowan woke Alice and whispered something before getting up and walking over.

The villager straightened and began to speak. "Yesterday a man came by and passed a message to the village's free tenants. Since my family and I are also free tenants, the man let me read what was written on the paper. I read it and looked at the man who brought it. 'This note isn't addressed to anyone,' I said."

The man only replied, 'They will know who it is.' With that response he kicked his mount and disappeared." The villager handed the folded paper to Peter. "This is the said note. Because we didn't know who it was addressed to, we thought it was of little importance."

Peter unfolded the paper, noting the short, hasty writing. This was obviously written in a rush, not a care in any letter drawn. Shock and rage built up in Peter's veins as he read.

If you wish to see your child again, you must pay for her with blood. Without it consider your precious baby dead.

Peter felt finger's grip his shoulder in a tight, constricted manner. He heard Charlotte's breathing quicken beside him. Clearly she had read the message over his shoulder. Looking at him with a gaze of sheer panic she remarked, "Peter, it's a ransom note."

"Yes, love, I know," Peter replied. He forced his voice to remain steady despite his own panic running through his veins. It was no use letting her know he was nervous. Rowan grunted from his position near the other expectant knights, waiting to see what was penned on the paper. Peter looked down at his boots then back at Rowan and surrendered the note to his steward's hands. The knights leaned into Rowan, reading it with him. Rowan and the knight's eyes slowly raised to Peter's.

"My king this is...this is a ransom," Rowan said. He looked at it again as if willing the note to say more. "But, where...where are we supposed to go? There is no location."

"I know, Rowan," Peter answered. "I have to think."

"What is it, dear?" Alice's soft voice asked from the tree. "Is it a note that says where we will find our children?"

Rowan exchanged a broken glance with Peter. Peter could barely imagine what it would be like to have to break news like this to an already devastated wife. At times like these, he was thankful Charlotte remained strong. Even though he knew inside her was a war of emotions.

"No, dear, there is no location," Rowan said. He continued in a stammering manner, "It's a...it's a...er...ransom note."

A wail escaped Alice's mouth and she fell against the tree. Rowan rushed to her side and knelt down, allowing her to throw her arms around his neck. "Rowan! Oh, little Faye and Gavin! Oh, my poor children!"

Peter watched as Charlotte knelt beside her friend and put a hand on Alice's shoulder. "We'll find your children, Alice. Whoever has Myla has Gavin and Faye." Charlotte's gaze rested on Peter, "We're one step closer," she said, willing him to confirm her statement.

Peter only nodded, not wanting to bring Alice's hopes down any more than they already were. But, in him, he knew he needed to remain realistic with Rowan and the rest of the group. They couldn't raise their hopes too high or risk the chance of them being dashed again. "I'll speak some more with this villager. Perhaps we'll learn something more."

Charlotte left Rowan to comfort Alice and trotted up to Peter, gripping his arm with icy fingers. "We aren't any closer are we, Peter?" she asked in a low voice.

"No Charlotte. Without any direction we are lost," he replied. "But, I have faith that this villager might know more."

She nodded and followed him over to where the villager stood with the other knights.

"I must question you more on this matter," Peter began.

The man bowed his head, "Oh course, my king. Ask anything you please, for I am your servant."

"Before I begin, I would like to know your name," Peter said. "I may need to call upon you in the future."

"It's Mark," the man responded. "Mark of Felstead."

"Well then, Mark," Peter said. "It occurred to me that this village you refer to as Felstead was scouted entirely by my knights. If you knew of a ransom note that led to my daughter, why not tell one of them?"

"With all due respect, my king, we didn't feel the note was important. It had no name or address. Like I said before, the man told us the people who found it would know it was directed to them."

Peter looked up to the sky and ran a hand down his face. "Do you find this note important now, Mark?"

"I'm afraid so," Mark said, hanging his head. "Forgive me for not taking note of the message scrawled on the paper. I now understand Aurum's future is in jeopardy."

"You're forgiven," Peter said. "Do not blame yourself too hard. You had no notion of what this was to mean. Just see that you don't pass over something this suspicious next time."

"Yes, my king," Mark replied. "I will not make such a foolish mistake again."

"But, do you by any chance know where these men were headed?" Peter asked. This was the one question he longed to have an answer for. Their chances of finding Myla depended on this villager's observation.

"But Peter," Charlotte spoke up suddenly, "This man told us the note was passed on in yesterday's daylight. Myla was kidnapped at night."

"You have a point, my love," Peter answered, hiding his disappointment that culprits wouldn't be headed back to where they came from.

"Our lovely queen is correct," Mark said. "The man who dropped the message off met up with more men on the roadside and galloped off towards the Royal fortress."

"Then the kidnappers dispatched the message before taking my daughter," Peter observed. He grunted. "It's a clever card to play really. It's more likely to confuse someone and make it seem of little importance if the message has no clear address and the event hasn't happened yet."

"Or perhaps it is not a ransom note for Myla after all," Charlotte ventured. But, as she exchanged a glance with Peter, he knew she didn't believe her own words. Even if there was a possibility of the fact being true, it was slim. The connection between the two events happening in the same day and the wording of the note was no coincidence. It was planned. Peter tried to come from a different angle, "Do you know where these men came from?"

"Yes, my king," Mark answered.

Peter looked to each of his knights. Now they were getting somewhere.

"It was easy to tell, for you do not smell this odor here. They smelled of salt. This means they could only come from one area. The sea, they came from the sea."

The dread that had already filled Peter plummeted to his stomach. If the culprits had come from the sea, that vast expanse of water, Myla could be anywhere. The ocean was the one part of this earth that Peter was unfamiliar with. Aurum was nowhere near any large bodies of water, giving Peter the major disadvantage of not knowing the ocean or how to navigate on it. He managed a nod to Mark. "Thank you. You've helped in a way of giving us a hint as to where the princess can be found." Peter fished out another few shillings from his pocket and dropped them into Mark's hand, "For any inconvenience we have given you."

Mark looked at the silver coins then returned his gaze to Peter. "Thank you, my king. And may God go with you."

Peter nodded, "Thank you."

Once Mark had left, Peter turned to his group to discuss further plans. "It seems our plans have changed due to our new route," Peter began. "The journey will not require all of us. Sir William, Sir Gilbert, and Sir Adam, you will be returning to my fortress with the new mare I purchased. I also wish for you to report back to Lord Edmund and Lord Geoffrey that they will be running the kingdom until we return."

The knights nodded their consent.

Peter continued, "Simon you are to remain with me and Rowan. And Rowan, your wife is to..." he trailed off and looked at Charlotte. With his eyes, he begged for her to turn back with Alice. He didn't want to drag his sick wife across an ocean and into an unknown land. Charlotte frowned. She knew what he was thinking and she had given him her answer with that one scowl. Peter sighed, "Your wife will continue along with Queen Charlotte."

Charlotte smiled her approval at his decision and hurried over to Luna, who was napping nearby. With a growl of protest the beast got up and let Charlotte saddle her.

Peter broke up the group and allowed each to make preparations for their separate journeys. As he checked his own courser, he heard another one of Charlotte's hoarse coughs. He turned to see her leaning against Luna, her hand over her mouth. Guilt filled Peter and he knew he should have ordered Charlotte to return home for her own welfare, because this journey would hold everything but safety.

Chapter 8

Peter dismounted from his courser and read the sign above the whitewashed building. The Cerulean Inn. Peter looked around him, taking in the bustling ocean town. With the shining blue water hugging them from three angles, the town's name, Cerulean, was appropriate. As was the white, lime washed buildings with their dark wooden frames, contrasting with the ocean.

Charlotte slipped off Luna and guided her along with Ferox to Peter's side. He watched in amusement as the townsfolk gasped in surprise at the huge creatures and hurried away. He'd noticed many times when they were on the road that the few people they passed switched to the other side of the road, avoiding the beasts with wide eyes. Charlotte looked up at him, "Are we stopping here? Should we not look for a ship?"

Peter smiled. Even if her stubbornness about coming vexed him, her persistence amazed him to no end. In truth, he would rather have her by his side than anyone else. "We will look for passage in time, love. You and Alice need your rest. We've been on the road for hours and with your health, you need some rest."

Charlotte gave him a defiant glare. "Have I not told you, Peter? My health is fine?" A cough escaped her lips at the end of her statement.

"Ah, you see," Peter said, glad to prove her wrong for once, "your body doesn't agree. No, you need to rest."

"But, Peter we need to..."

"I will look around for a ship that might lead to the thieves and children. It is safer for you and Alice to stay here, anyway."

Charlotte sighed, "Fine. At least all of us won't be idle."

As they entered the dim interior of the inn, an old man Peter assumed to be the innkeeper hobbled towards them. "How may I serve you, good people?"

"We need three rooms, my good man," Peter said, stepping forward.

"Ah, yes, of course." The man seemed to take note of Peter's attire and sword hilt. "You are of noble birth, I see."

Having left all of their royal emblems with the returning knights, Peter wanted to remain as unnoticeable as any common man. But, with his sword's gleaming hilt, along with his wife's treasured griffins, one could easily see they at least had noble blood. Peter decided it was best if he led the man on to believe they were passing nobles, not the man's ruling monarchs. It was less likely to be leaked to unwanted ears. "Yes, you are correct. We are on our way to my relative's wedding and we need a place to lay our heads before we carry on."

"Well, my lords, you have come to the right place." He gestured to Charlotte, "Due to your noble status and the women, I think you want large rooms?"

Peter looked to Charlotte then to the rest of the group. Rowan nodded his approval, while Simon shrugged as if it didn't matter. Peter turned back to the innkeeper. "Yes, large rooms will serve us fine."

With a nod, the innkeeper hobbled off to find the right keys.

———————

After settling Charlotte into their room and making sure the griffins were safely hidden in the inn's stables, Peter strode through the crowds with Rowan and Simon behind, heading for the port. The sun was starting to die in the sky, painting the sky a sea of violent colors. It had taken him some more time to convince Charlotte to stay put and look in on Alice once in a while. She had had a sharp retort but when he reminded her that she'd given her word to listen to him, she reluctantly agreed. If they were to find passage across the ocean tomorrow they had to hurry.

Peter could taste the salt in the air and the smell of the port's murky water sickened his stomach. To think sailors and their captains endured this acrid air every day nauseated him. He would never grow accustomed to ocean life. Raised inland, he was a foreign man in this town. Huge ships with their towering masts loomed ahead of him, casting their skinny shadows in ragged lines on the loose, cobblestone pathway.

As they stopped near a ship on the creaky dock, Peter noticed even more alarming details. Rotting wood held the massive ships in place, along with a frayed rope underwater. Peter could only hope that the rope would hold the ship in place and not snap off the anchor, since the rotted wood wouldn't lend a hand. Sailors walked to and fro around them, hauling goods off ships and stacking them next to the rickety boards they walked on.

Peter turned to his group. They both had the same shocked expression as him and he could guess they both were thinking the same thing as him. Peter grunted and began, hoping to distract them from the sight around them. "We will cover more ground if we split up. See if any of the sailors know anything about a group of...men who boarded a ship to..." he trailed off. They didn't know where the thieves were headed. Without direction, they were lost. They'd hit a dead end, making the problem of finding clues expand in size.

Rowan seemed to read his thoughts. "We understand, er...my lord," he said, stumbling over his words, from not using the term 'lord' for over two years.

Peter shook his head, "No, Rowan. You must call me by my name. I don't want the wrong people to assume we're nobility. The fewer people who know us to have noble blood the better. I don't want to attract the wrong attention."

"Of course, Peter," Simon answered. "Should we meet back here afterwards?"

"Yes. After you have spoken to all the sailors or, better yet, the captains and first mates, meet back here by this ship." Peter peered at the faded name on the ship's side, "The *Ventus Amicus.*"

"Agreed," Simon and Rowan answered.

Splitting up, Peter watched as Rowan jogged to the right and Simon to the left. With his men speaking to the sailors, Peter decided to speak to the merchants and traders at the port. Being here all day and every day to make sales, they would definitely see everyone who boarded.

Charlotte sat curled up in the darkest corner of her room and let the sobs wrack her body. After the hours of traveling and hiding her raging emotions behind her stone walls, when Peter left, she let herself fall apart on the stone floor, heartache running through her veins and escaping from her body in sobs. All the loss since that night fell into her cries: her fears for her daughter's safety and Alice's children, and her own foolishness for not having a guard with Alice and the children that night. If only she'd looked ahead and made sure everything was secure, before she let Gavin take Myla away. If only she had seen what was to come. But that was it. She would never see into the future. She would always remain ignorant of what was to come.

A cough rose in her throat with the sobs. She felt the moist saliva shoot out of her mouth with the air. Bile rose in her throat and made her lean against the wall. She couldn't help but notice she was growing more and more ill every passing day. Alice had been giving her herbs to help with the coughing, but the illness seemed reluctant to leave the home it had made in her body. She groaned, that's just what she needed. A sickness that would make Peter regret taking her along, thinking she was just a burden. No, she could not get sicker. For her daughter's sake, she needed to remain strong like the stone queen her people knew her to be.

A door creaking open startled her and made her jerk her head up.

"Charlotte?" a familiar voice called out. Concern was in every word he mouthed. She remembered then that Peter couldn't see her. Perhaps he wouldn't see her crumpled and broken form on the floor. She concealed her cries for another time and stood up. Voicing her surprise she asked, "Peter, what are you doing here?"

He surveyed the room. "Charlotte, where are you. Come out here where I can see you."

She stepped into the dim light. Dread filled her as her face illuminated in the lantern's light.

Peter moved forward the second she came out. He stood before her, relief washing over his features. Then, frowning, he asked, "You have been crying." He touched her tear streaked face, tracing the lines with his fingertips.

Charlotte feigned a surprised face, "Crying? I wasn't…"

He lifter a finger to her lips. "Do you dare try to deceive me, Charlotte? You can't lie to me. The evidence is right before my eyes."

She shook her head. New drops fell from her lashes. She was losing to her emotions with him. No, this couldn't happen.

Peter swiped the new droplets away with care and gazed down at her with his loving, blue eyes. "It's about Myla is it not?" he asked in a whisper.

Charlotte could only nod. Her emotions took over and she began to weep softly. She scolded herself. She'd vowed not to cry in front of her husband. She'd never wanted to have him burdened by a soft wife. She could look out for herself and he wouldn't need to waste his time on her. But, she found herself speaking through her cries. "She's so little, Peter. I can't imagine what my child is enduring right now. It seems impossible how she could live through this. And Gavin and little Faye too. They all must be terrified."

"I know," Peter soothed. "I can't imagine any of that either. But we are doing all we can. We just have to remain focused and strong."

There, the last statement. He was making fun of her weakness. This was the time to show him she could be just as strong without anyone. She pulled away from his touch with such force, it surprised Peter. "So be it. If we are to be strong then I won't let my worries defeat me and won't toss them on your shoulders, you have enough to worry about without me."

Peter took her hand as she tried to walk away. Warmth shot up her arm, making her turn to face him again. "Charlotte, you don't have to act like this," he soothed, "please come here."

She let out a ragged breath. "What, Peter?" she asked. Better make him say what he wants to say then ask him to leave. "Make it quick," she managed to snap.

"I only want to comfort you," he revealed, his voice the very sound of innocence. "Is that too much to ask? You reject my comfort whenever I offer it to you."

"I don't reject it," she retorted, tugging her hand from his grasp. "I simply don't need it. It makes me feel weak."

Peter sighed, "It's all right to accept comfort, Charlotte."

When she was about to protest, he pulled her into his arms and swayed her back and forth. She felt him nuzzling into her hair and his arm stroking her back, sending tingles up her spine. She could feel it all the way into her heart. His love was like a knife carving its way into her stone walls. Pretty soon they would fall if she didn't push him away. "Peter..." she mumbled, her voice muffled by his chest.

"What, my love?"

His name for her was too much. She felt the walls tumble down and she began to sob uncontrollably. Peter continued to rock her back and forth, all the time stroking her back and murmuring soothing words to her aching heart. "I just want her back," she said through her cries. "I just want my child back, Peter."

Peter kissed the top of her head and continued to hold her close. "I know, love. I want her back too. Myla is everything I ever wanted in a child. She reminds me of her strong willed mother."

Charlotte stopped crying for a moment, the statement decreasing her sobs to sniffles. She looked up at him with wet green eyes. "Truly?" she asked, wondering if he actually said such a thing or if it was a figment of her imagination.

Peter smiled and kissed her lips, sending a wave of warmth through her. "Truly," he answered. Frowning he said, "Don't you ever doubt that."

She could only nod and look up into his sincere, deep, blue eyes.

"Have you found us passage across the sea?" she whispered, breaking the peaceful silence.

Peter's eyes filled with sorrow and Charlotte dreaded his answer. "We don't know where the thieves took Myla. We have no sense of direction from here. I spoke with some merchants who visit the port daily to make sales, but they see too many people coming and going they wouldn't recognize one from another." He sighed. "I'm sorry, Charlotte. I know you wanted me to find us a ship to cross on but..." he trailed off, diverting his gaze, his voice broken.

Charlotte laid a hesitant hand on his cheek, making him look into her eyes. "We can only hope and pray something happens that will lead us to Myla," she began. "But, I learned from experience that you never give up, no matter what stands in your way. If that is an ocean, then I will sail the whole earth to find my daughter. I'm not afraid of the future and you shouldn't be either."

Peter smiled. "You have a way with words that keeps my hopes up." He clasped her hand holding his cheeks and pressed a kiss to it. "Never lose that quality."

"I won't, Peter. It's who I am."

A knock at the door made her jerk away from Peter. He seemed to understand her want of space when others were around and stepped away. "Who's knocking?" he asked.

"It's Simon!" came a voice full of triumph.

Peter opened the door and revealed a fidgeting, young knight. "Yes, Simon. What news? Surely it's good, if you can't stand still."

"Oh, most excellent news, Peter!" he exclaimed. "I found us passage on a ship. Tomorrow at dawn we set sail on the *Ventus Amicus*."

Chapter 9

"Welcome aboard, my good people!" A stoic man announced from the deck. Peter mounted the gangplank and walked across to shake the man's hand. "You must be the captain."

"That I am," the man replied, helping Alice over the ship's entrance. After escorting her over and making sure she was steady on the rocking floorboards, Peter watched as the captain came to Charlotte's aid next. She looked from him to Peter before accepting his waiting hand. Walking over the gangplank, she walked straight to Peter's side. He slipped his hand into hers to reassure her and watched the captain shake Rowan and Simon's hands before turning to all of them. "I am Captain Sadon! It is an honor to be commanding this vessel that is carrying our great king and," he bowed to Charlotte, "our lovely queen."

Charlotte only nodded in response. As she met Peter's gaze, confusion swarmed in her eyes. She wasn't the only one. Peter found himself lost for words. How did the captain know they were the royal family? They hadn't revealed that fact to anyone in this town, even the inn keeper thought they were just nobility. He'd have to speak with Simon about this. "We are grateful to you, captain, for allowing us to sail with you. But, may I speak with one of my knights in private for a moment?"

"Of course, my king." Captain Sadon gestured to an unaccompanied corner of the ship. "Please, no one shall bother you there."

Peter nodded, "Thank you, captain." He caught Simon's eye and jerked his head toward the corner. Simon followed him like a criminal on his way to the gallows. Reaching the corner, Peter swung around at him and hissed, "How does he know we are the royal family?"

Simon shifted his weight from one foot to another. Scratching behind his ear and avoiding Peter's gaze he said, "I told him, Peter."

Peter nodded. He'd expected that. "But, why?" he asked. "You know that I wanted to remain unnoticed."

"Peter, I wasn't getting anywhere simply asking if they'd seen any strange men boarding a ship in a hurry. The sailors don't take notice of their passengers or cargo very well." Simon looked across at Captain Sadon then back at Peter. "I decided to ask the captain if he'd seen anyone try to smuggle a child aboard a ship."

"And?" Peter probed.

"He said he didn't know. He said he was a busy man and didn't pay attention to everything being loaded on other ships because he had his own to worry about." Simon sighed, "That's when I told him I was a knight for the king and that the princess was kidnapped."

"What did he say then?" Peter asked.

"He said he had heard about the princess' kidnapping and he offers his condolences. When I told him we were looking for her, he perked up. He said he'd seen some men head off to a town with a bundle in their arms. He couldn't be sure what was in the bundle but he swore he thought it was a child."

"And where was this ship headed?"

"A town by the name of Perdita."

"And that's where we're headed now?"

"Yes, Peter, of course. Do you really believe the captain would steer us off course? He said he'd do anything for the king and queen. Especially if Aurum's future is in jeopardy."

Peter sighed, "Very well, Simon. You seem to know more than me. I never thanked you for finding us passage and I should. Thank you."

"Your welcome, Peter. I would do anything for Aurum. My loyalty will never falter again."

Peter smiled, remembering Simon's past experience with shifting loyalty. The queen had charged him with treason and, only through Peter, would she consider sparing his life. To Peter, Simon seemed to be trying to prove himself to them and making up for his unfaithfulness. "I know it won't, Simon. You have worked hard and diligently and are a worthy knight. You've proven yourself once again."

Walking back over to the group clustered around the captain, Peter announced, "Captain, I would like to see where we will be staying. What rooms are ours?"

"Yes, yes!" Captain Sadon said. He gestured for them to follow. "Come, I shall show you."

The clash of swords echoed across the ship. Peter sparred with Simon on the deck of the *Ventus Amicus*, practicing his swordsmanship. But, what Peter craved more than practice was the fresh salt air. Despite their cabins below deck having plenty of room, they were stuffy and too warm in the afternoon. As long as they kept their distance from the working sailors, they were allowed on deck.

Alice worked on stitching a square of fabric, while Rowan stood next to her watching the ocean. Charlotte stood on Alice's other side, but instead of watching the ocean or embroidering, she was transfixed on Peter and Simon's mock dual.

Simon swiped at Peter's collarbone, making Peter dodge the blow and attack Simon before he could recover from his swing. Hacking at the young knight's sword, Peter gave him little time to defend, let alone attack Peter back. After a few more minutes, Simon backed away from Peter and held up his hands. "I surrender, Peter. I shall faint if I continue."

Peter cocked a brow, about to play with Simon's nerves. But, seeing the knight dripping in sweat and breathing in gasps through his mouth, he conceded not to. Instead, he let Simon sink down by the deck's side and turned toward Rowan. "Want to try to best your king, Rowan?"

Rowan shook his head, "Oh no, my king. I could never best you. You know very well that I am no match for you in swords."

"May I try?" Charlotte asked, a smile playing on her lips.

Peter let the idea run through his mind. Charlotte's coughing wasn't clearing and, if he was correct, it was getting worse.

"I'm not sure that's such a good idea, Charlotte," Alice remarked, voicing Peter's concern. "You coughing has grown worse."

Charlotte frowned. "I'm fine," she retorted. Glaring at Peter she challenged, "Well?"

He raked a hand through his hair and looked from Charlotte to Alice. Alice's eyes were wide and seemed to plead with Charlotte not to do anything foolish, while Charlotte's glare told him she was confident and didn't want to back down. He shrugged and gestured for Charlotte to come to the center. She beamed and picked up her sword she'd propped by her side. "But," Peter warned, pointing a finger at her, "if you start to feel uneasy and tired, you tell me and we'll stop."

"Fine," she said, "but, I'll prove you all wrong. I'm just as strong as I was when I left home."

Alice seemed about to protest one last time, but shut her mouth after seeing Charlotte's glare in her direction. Charlotte turned back to Peter and raised her sword and readied her stance.

"Ready?" Peter asked, bracing himself.

Instead of responding, Charlotte launched herself at him, bringing her sword near his side.

Peter blocked and swung at her legs.

She jumped and landed to the side of him, taking an aim at his ribs. He retreated backwards and readied himself to attack again. But, Charlotte continued advancing towards him, hacking at each of his sides. He warded off the blows and looked for an opening in which to strike, but found none.

His wife's swift attacks would forever amaze him. For having such a slim frame no one would expect her to put up a good fight. But that she did. She watched her enemy with those blazing eyes and never retreated, she only pushed forward. In Peter's eyes she was a true beauty in both features and talent. And she always would be.

Charlotte faked a few blows at his ribs then swung to catch him off guard by his neck. Peter blocked then took advantage of his height. Her blows had been high and it had taken awhile for her to bring her arm down. He aimed a blow at her side, but she blocked it and went for his legs. He side stepped her blows and came at her again.

But, instead of blocking, Charlotte fell to the ground, her sword clattering a few steps away. Peter had knocked it right out of her hand. Retching coughs shook her frame from head to foot.

"Charlotte!" Peter exclaimed, dropping next to her.

Her coughing didn't stop, it only grew worse. Peter could hear the mucus in her throat and knew she wasn't well. She hadn't been well since that day when he'd reluctantly brought her along. She just feigned wellness and pushed on, despite her growing sickness.

"Charlotte!" Alice screamed. She knelt by Peter and turned her friend over. "Oh, why didn't I stop you," Alice muttered. "I'm a fool."

Peter shook his head. Alice wasn't the fool. He was. He scooted to where Charlotte's head lay on the boards and propped it up, cradling it with his arms. Charlotte moaned and covered her mouth, smothering a harsh cough. When her hands fell away, Peter's heart skipped a beat. Her mouth was tinged red. Charlotte never was one to wear painted lips except for parties. Looking at her hands, Peter saw what he'd dreaded. He heard Alice gasp beside him. "Is that..." he trailed off, not wanting it to be true.

"Yes, my king," Alice said. She met his gaze with worried eyes. "It's blood."

Peter could only nod. Blood. No, it couldn't be. Let it be anything but blood. No! He bowed his head and laid it against Charlotte's forehead. "No," he whispered.

"My queen?"

Peter looked up to see Simon standing over him, with Rowan right beside him. Concern was on both their faces, and for a good reason.

"She needs to be moved to her room, my king," Alice said, breaking the silence. "I can try to give her some herbs there."

Peter nodded and stood up. Bending down, he hoisted Charlotte up, cradling her in his arms. She only moaned and tucked her head near his shoulder. A cough racked her body, making Peter hasten to their room. If she was coughing blood, her life could easily be on the line.

"We can only pray, my king," Alice said, packing her herbs into her bag. "I don't have many herbs left. My supplies have dwindled since we left port. My cough medicine is the worst, I don't have much left."

Peter nodded from where he sat next to Charlotte on their bed. She'd fallen into a restless sleep in his arms and they'd had to wake her up to give her Alice's herb remedy. "Hopefully the herbs help, Alice," he said.

"That's the problem, my king," Alice replied. "I've been giving our queen the coughing herbs since we left, but it hasn't killed the virus yet. It's strange, for the herbs are supposed to at least ease the pain. They did, but it didn't last long."

"Do you suppose it's a different illness?" Peter asked.

"I cannot say, my king," Alice answered. Looking down she added, "I've never treated anyone who was coughing up blood. Surely my mother had, but she never let me near her patients when the illnesses they had were contagious."

Peter put an arm around Charlotte's head. "Do you suppose..."

"I don't know, my king. Like I said, I have never seen anyone spit blood."

Peter nodded. "I see."

Rowan came to the open door and looked in.

Peter just shook his head.

Bowing his head, Rowan looked down at his boots.

Peter nodded to Rowan, "Go with your husband, Alice. I'll call you in if she wakes up."

"Of course my king," Alice said, picking her bag up. Rising, she hurried to Rowan's side and hugged him as he guided her away.

Peter rested his head against Charlotte's. Her eyes flickered but remained closed. He yearned to drink in her green gaze, those beautiful eyes that always made his heart hammer against his chest. Peter scolded himself again for his recklessness. *Fool! Why did you let her practice? You caused this, you caused her illness to worsen! What kind of husband are you?*

He swept a stray hair from Charlotte's forehead. "I'm sorry, my love," he whispered. "I caused this, and I don't deserve you. I'm a fool." He pressed a kiss to her forehead and added, "With all my power, Charlotte, I will do everything I can to make this better."

———————

A crack of thunder split the air, roaring across the vast ocean. Waves larger than castle walls tossed the ship around like a child tossing a ball. Lightening shot through the air, blinding the sailors as they struggled with the sails.

Peter steadied himself against the wall of his cabin, trying to reach the door. His legs were still adjusting to walking onboard. It was late in the night when he'd been awakened by the loud, crashing thunder. Charlotte hadn't awoken; only moaned or tossed and turned in fitful sleep.

Peter looked back to where Charlotte slept. He needed to reach the door and ask the captain if they were going to go down. He couldn't bare to leave Charlotte, especially in her ill state. But, he needed to know if they would survive.

He stumbled across the room and leaned against the door while another wave swept the ship along like a toy. Jerking it open when the wave passed, he fell into the tight hall, crashing against the opposite wall.

"King Peter!" a shout echoed from next to him. The yell was almost inaudible in the storm and if the man hadn't been next to him, Peter knew he wouldn't have heard him.

He turned towards the voice to find the first mate, Giles, standing next to him. "Giles!" Peter shouted back at him. "I need to speak with the captain!" his voice drowned out in the storm.

Giles shook his head, "No, my king! You must stay in the cabin! Captain Sadon ordered me to keep you and the rest of the passengers in their rooms! You are not to leave the cabins!"

"But I must know if we are to survive! Or are we to become part of the sea?" Peter yelled.

"My king, you don't need to worry about that!" Giles replied. "Now, get back in that cabin before you kill yourself!"

"Answer me, Giles! Are we going to sink?"

"Get in the cabin!" bellowed Giles. "We can't afford to lose our kingdom's monarch!"

Peter glared at the first mate a while longer. The man's firm, brown eyes made Giles' decision clear. He would reveal nothing to his passengers. Peter's shoulders sank and he returned to his cabin, shutting the door behind him.

Another wave swept the ship up, making Peter fall against his bed. Steadying himself, he sat against the flat pillows and closed his eyes. His head was beginning to spin from the constant tipping of the ship. The last thing he needed was to suffer from   sea sickness. A jerk told him the wall of water was bringing them crashing down. He gripped the bed to prevent himself from toppling off.

Charlotte rolled against him and he felt her body jerk. Without warning, she sat up, her eyes wide. She let out a cough that was muffled by the thunder. Through the lightning, he saw a spot of blood on her hand. He grabbed the cloth Alice had given him and thrust it into Charlotte's hands. She covered her mouth and fell against him. He hugged her close and braced himself for the next massive wave.

The storm continued throughout the whole night and into the morning. No sun was visible and dark clouds covered the sky, blackening the only source of light they had. Peter waited in agony for the storm to finish it's raging fit. He was beginning to get impatient and yearned for the fresh air on deck. Not only that, but Charlotte's forehead was heating up with surprising speed. He'd stripped the covers off of her to cool her off but she still remained warm. Stranger yet, with the covers off she had broken into a sweat, her hair clinging to her damp skin. She'd woken only once more with chills and insisted on covering herself up. But, not long after she fell back into a fitful sleep, Peter had tossed the covers aside. There was no questioning that Charlotte's illness was growing worse. He needed to reach Alice — and fast.

The door burst open and a shadow of a man loomed in front of it. Peter reached for his dagger, ready to defend Charlotte and himself if needed. The storm would be the perfect cover for a thieving sailor to plunder a few possessions.

The figure held up his hands. He must have seen Peter's quick movement and the glint of the knife between the flashes of lightening. "My king, it's me!" the man said.

Peter recognized the voice. Captain Sadon. "Captain!" Peter shouted back. "When is the storm going to end? My wife is ill and may be on the verge of dying! I need to get her to her maid! She's the one who can cure her!"

"I know, King Peter!" the captain replied. "I found out from your steward! I'm here to take you and the queen to a safer cabin. The queen's maid is waiting there."

Relief flooded Peter. Bracing himself for the ship's swaying motion, he stood up. He slipped his arms underneath Charlotte, making her moan. She opened and shut her eyes, as if trying to focus. "Shhh, Charlotte. I'm taking you to Alice," Peter soothed near her ear. "She's going to give you more herbs."

Charlotte gave a weak nod and shut her eyes, allowing Peter to cradle her in his arms. With her added weight, he found it difficult to balance. He stumbled and would have fallen if the captain hadn't caught him by the shoulder and helped support him.

Slowly, the captain led them to a bigger room set higher up than the rest. Peter climbed the few steps up to the door and the captain opened it for them. Alice and Rowan sat in one corner on a bench, clinging to each other. Captain Sadon pointed to a bed and Peter carried Charlotte over to it and laid her down. She didn't wake at all. Peter shot Alice a worried look. Rowan steadied Alice as she walked over to Peter and began peering into her bag of herbs. "I need water, captain," she told Captain Sadon. "Without water, the queen won't be able to swallow the medicine."

Captain Sadon nodded and hurried out of the room. Alice turned back to searching through her bag. Pulling out a bunch of green leaves she began to roll them around on her fingers. "I can make the medicine once the captain returns."

"What's wrong with Charlotte?" Peter shot out.

Alice put a hand on his and said, "She has a fever, my king. I must break it before anything else. These are coriander leaves, they'll help break the fever."

After Captain Sadon returned it didn't take long before Alice had made the herb mixture. Peter lifted Charlotte to a seated position, waking her. She blinked and squinted. She coughed, sending mucus with blood out of her mouth. Alice dabbed Charlotte's mouth with a cloth and said, "Charlotte, my sister, you must drink this. You have a fever and some other illness I have yet to define. Please, drink..." she trailed off and held the cup to Charlotte's lips. Her mouth opened and she began to swallow the medicine. She frowned and shoved the cup away with the little strength she had and shook her head. Alice observed the cup's remains. "She drank half," she announced. When Peter was about to protest, she added, "A good amount, my king. I shall come back to check on her later. If she should wake again, have her finish the rest of the cup."

Peter nodded and watched as Captain Sadon, Rowan, and Alice left him to watch over Charlotte. Making himself comfortable on the new bed, he held her close, making sure she didn't fall off.

When she woke a couple of hours later, Peter offered the rest of the medicine to her. She accepted it and finished it off. Cracking a small smile, she mouthed a 'thank you' then closed her eyes once again.

Peter leaned his head against the bed's headboard and closed his eyes. Sending a silent prayer up to the heavens, he fell into a restless sleep.

Chapter 10

The storm finally relinquished its power and abandoned them by the end of the second day. Being able to walk out on the deck in the fresh air comforted Peter. But, his comforts cascaded to the pit of his stomach when Alice told him of Charlotte's health that morning. Her fever was still clinging to her stubbornly, along with chills and coughs racking her body. Alice tried everything in her power to improve Charlotte's health, but no medicine seemed to treat her symptoms. Worse yet, Alice's herbs were dwindling rapidly.

Peter stared out at the horizon, letting the wind buffet his hair as he watched the sunset. If only his worries could be freed as easily as the wind.

"My king?"

He whirled around and came face to face with the first mate. "Giles, I didn't hear you approach."

Giles shrugged, "You were busy with your thoughts, my king." Gesturing to the ship's interior he added, "I hate to interrupt, but the captain wishes to have an audience with your highness."

Peter nodded, "Of course."

Peter found Captain Sadon pacing to and fro in his cabin. Only when Giles grunted did the captain take note of their presence. "Oh, gentlemen, forgive me, I didn't see you. Please, come in," he said, urging them farther into the room.

Peter stepped in and Giles shut the door behind them. "Captain," Peter said, "you wanted to see me?"

"Yes, yes," Captain Sadon said, sitting down behind his desk. "How is the weather treating you now that the tempest has passed?"

Peter remembered the awful nausea he had experienced during the storm when the ship tossed and turned. No doubt his dinner had come up more than once. "My health is in good condition. I'm simply not used to such storms at sea. You know me to be raised on land."

Captain Sadon cracked a small smile. "Yes, my king. These storms take some getting used to. In time, you come to expect what comes with them." The captain paused and rubbed the back of his neck. "How is the queen faring? These past few days must have been awful for Her Majesty."

Peter's face fell, "No, she isn't any better. She's extremely ill."

"Do the new accommodations help with her comfort?" Captain Sadon asked.

"Yes," Peter replied, "This new room is treating us well. She is quite comfortable, as am I."

"You?" Giles asked, moving to stand beside the captain's desk.

"Yes," Peter answered, "I'm staying with my queen to make sure nothing life threatening happens."

Giles and the captain exchanged glances, seeming to pass a message Peter couldn't decipher. "Is she still coughing blood, my king?" Giles asked.

"Yes, first mate," Peter responded, annoyance rising, "she's still coughing blood."

"Do you know if the illness our queen has is contagious?" Captain Sadon asked.

"No," Peter answered. "Her maid is uncertain of what she has."

"Then I advise you to take another room, my king," Captain Sadon said. "If it's contagious, we can't run the risk of losing our monarch."

Peter frowned. They were instructing him to house in another room just because they were afraid of him dying? What of Charlotte? She was their monarch as well and even when they showed their concern, Peter's gut told him they cared more about his protection and health than hers. Well not him. No, he would stay where he pleased and if he ran the risk of catching Charlotte's disease so be it. He wanted to be near her at all times.

He broke the silence that had consumed them all for the past minute. "Captain, would you care to tell me when we are scheduled to dock in Perdita? The queen's maid is in need of new herbs and fears she'll run out before we reach land."

"If all goes well, we should dock in two days' time," Captain Sadon informed. "Do you think the herbs will hold out for at least that much longer?"

"I don't know, but I pray that it is so. If not..." Peter broke off and refused to dwell on the rising thoughts. "Never mind. I will not spoil a fine day with my stormy thoughts."

Captain Sadon nodded in understanding.

Clearing his throat, Peter added, "I'll leave you and Giles to your plans. I wish to check on our queen."

The captain exchanged another concerned look with Giles before replying, "Very well. It was a pleasure speaking with you, my king. Please, if there is anything either you or the queen need, let me know."

"I will, Captain. Thank you," Peter replied before making his way to Charlotte's room.

The bitter taste of blood filled Charlotte's mouth, making her spit it out. She groaned and rolled onto her side. After Alice had announced that her fever had broken mere minutes ago, Charlotte let her mind rejoice. She'd felt strength surge through her body after that. But, perhaps it had been the herbs Alice had given her? Either way, she felt more awake. But, with awareness came the consistent pain in her throat and the rough coughs that only made it worse. Her throat throbbed from coughing so much, while in truth she didn't remember most of it. Alice had told her she'd fallen asleep every time she woke up. She hadn't stayed fully awake for long periods of time.

Alice had ordered her to rest and not to get up. Her friend was taking extra precautions and, since Charlotte had no strength to speak, she yielded to Alice's requests.

But, if her own thoughts of what illness dwelled in her body were correct, she knew what she had. There was one sickness Alice was ignorant of, but she wasn't.

Alice's mother had had her hands full taking care of other patients that she had taken under her wing. Alice was away at the time so Charlotte had filled in to help Alice's mother. One patient was coughing blood, the disease Charlotte was sure she had. The patient had been close to dying and only recovered because, at the time, Alice's mother knew of an herb that could cure the disease. But, Alice had not been present to see it. Not long after that the family had died in the village fire, leaving Alice with no knowledge of that one specific herb. Only Charlotte knew. If only she could find a way to tell Alice what she needed. If only she could find the strength to speak. A wave of tiredness crashed over her and she felt her eyelids droop. As sleep swept over her, she was aware of a door creaking open.

———————

Peter found Charlotte on her side, sleeping. Closing the door quietly behind him, he made his way noiselessly across the floor. If she was sleeping soundly, he didn't wish to wake her. He placed a hand on her forehead. Relief washed over him. It was still damp with sweat, but the heat that used to radiate from her skin had died down. He wondered when her fever had broken. Alice hadn't complained, but staying up with her last night left Charlotte's maid tired. He didn't blame her for trying to catch up on her sleep.

He was about to leave Charlotte to sleep when her eyes flew open. She squinted up at him as if struggling to define who he was. "It's me, Charlotte," he whispered.

Seeming to recall his voice, she relaxed and gave a slight smile. She opened her mouth to say something, but he put a finger to her lips. "No, Charlotte," he soothed. "Don't try to speak when you haven't the strength."

She frowned, obviously upset with his order, but conceded. She pointed to the bedside table, gesturing to a cup. Picking it up, Peter noticed it to be Alice's herb concoction. "Are you certain you need more of this?" he asked. "Perhaps I should fetch Alice."

She only shook her head and continued to hold out her hand. Remembering Charlotte was also skilled with herbs, he gave the cup to her. She would know when she needed some. Instead of releasing the cup, he asked, "Should I help you sit up first?"

She shook her head. Letting go of the cup he still held, she put her hands flat against the bed and hoisted herself up. Peter raised his brows. She had that much strength? She took the cup from him and tipped it back, drinking. After finishing what was left, she swiped her mouth with her hand and laid back down. Weakly, she pulled the sheet over her and looked up at him.

Peter got up to leave, only to be stayed by her hand. He looked back down at her, "Yes, Charlotte?"

She patted the place where he'd just sat. Her voice came out in a cracked whisper. "Stay, Peter....please."

He could only nod and sit back down next to her. Her dull green eyes portrayed a look he had never seen in her gaze. Could it be fear? A new wave of sympathy overtook him and he could hear his mind railing at him again for his stupidity. Stroking hair away from her damp forehead he soothed, "I'll stay as long as you want me to, love. I'll never leave your side."

Alice stared out across the water. The gentle rocking of the ship soothed her worries and eased her mind. Soon though, the worry would return, for she would have to check up on Charlotte again. She pushed aside her fear for her beloved friend. She would worry about that when she was with Charlotte. The only problem was, she couldn't stop. Charlotte was constantly on her mind and her worries that she was missing something that would heal her never let her rest. She found herself pacing back and forth at times and searching her mind for the right herbs to use. But nothing showed. Logically, she was doing all she could. She was giving Charlotte the herbs to ease the coughing and the medicine to break her fever. She sent up a prayer of thanks again that at least Charlotte's fever had broken that day. Something had gone right for once.

A hand on her shoulder caused her to whip around. Rowan stood behind her and smiled. "I did not mean to frighten you, dear."

Alice smiled back and leaned against him, "I know that."

He came up beside her and wrapped an arm around her shoulders, shielding her from the chilling breeze. The sun was getting ready to sleep and surrender its power to the moon. As she leaned against her husband another thought that had plagued her every night came to mind; her beloved children, Gavin and Faye. A stray tear escaped her eye and slid down her cheek. She buried her head against Rowan and he pulled her closer. He seemed to know her thoughts and her need for comfort. She smiled in spite of her dismal thoughts.

Sometimes the best comfort wasn't dictated but came through silent understanding and gestures. She brought her gaze back to the flaming sky. A silhouette of another ship came into view on the horizon. "Rowan, dear. Look, another ship," she remarked.

"Yes, dear, I see." She caught her husband frowning at the silhouette. He brought a hand to his forehead and peered into the distance.

"Perhaps we can ask if they have seen anyone who might have carried children across the sea?" she ventured.

Rowan turned to her and cracked a smile. She could tell, however, that it was forced. "Yes, perhaps."

"Rowan," a voice said behind them.

Alice turned with her husband and looked to see the first mate and Simon striding towards them. The men wore grim expressions and unease settled in her heart.

"Yes, Giles?" Rowan asked.

"I want you and your wife to make your way below deck," Giles replied.

"May I ask why?" Rowan questioned.

"Simon noted the ship on the horizon and my gut tells me it isn't a friendly visit," Giles replied. "Now, please hurry. This could be bloody."

Alice gasped. Rowan tugged her close to him and she took comfort that he was there with her. "Who do you suppose they are?" she dared to ask.

"Pirates."

––––––––––––

Simon hurried to the king's cabin. The threat of a pirate attack was fresh in his mind. Giles had warned him to watch the horizon for ships before they set sail. Simon had nodded but hadn't taken an invasion seriously until now. A pirate attack was going to be quite a story to tell his fellow knights when he returned.

He rapped his knuckles against the cabin's door. "Who's there?" Peter's voice came from inside.

"Simon," he answered.

The door opened, revealing a very tired version of Peter. Simon sympathized with the king. He knew Peter hadn't slept well last night, instead he had tended to the queen with Alice. This news would probably lower his spirits even more. "Peter, Giles spotted a ship on the horizon."

Peter cocked a brow as if wondering what was so important about another ship.

"Peter, it's not flying any colors. It's a pirate ship and Giles expects it to make an assault."

Peter's eyes lit up with new interest. "A pirate ship? Giles is positive?"

"Yes, I'm afraid so," Simon replied. "We're preparing to defend the ship."

Peter frowned. "What are you not revealing to me, Simon? I can tell you aren't speaking everything you know."

Could Peter truly read him that easily? He sighed. He might as well tell him. "Giles requests that you remain in your cabin. He doesn't want to risk..."

"Of course he doesn't!" Peter interrupted, making Simon jump. "Simon, Giles might mean well but he apparently doesn't think I can defend myself. I'll contribute to defending the assault as much as any other man."

"But, Peter, should you not stay here with the queen?" Simon asked, looking over his shoulder at Charlotte. He was surprised to find the queen watching the exchange. Her green eyes, though dull, were set on him, understanding every word.

Peter turned to look at Charlotte. He and the queen seemed to communicate silently until Peter turned back to him. "No, Simon. The queen is fine. The women will be fine as long as they are kept out of sight until the attack passes. I will join arms and fight with my life."

His eyes blazed with determination and Simon knew better than to contradict him. "Very well, Peter. But you will need to explain yourself to Giles."

"Let me handle the first mate, Simon," Peter replied. "There is only so far he can go before he is defying his king. And that, I guarantee you, he does not wish to do."

———

"King Peter!"

Peter whipped around to find Captain Sadon striding towards him, a frown creased on his brows. He crossed his arms, prepared to meet the captain head on.

"What in all the world are you doing out in the open?" the captain fired. He gestured wildly to the approaching ship. "Do you not see what danger you are in?"

"I see quite clearly, captain," Peter replied, "and I am prepared to face our enemy. You will not keep me locked away like a precious jewel. No, Captain, I plan to fight."

Captain Sadon muttered under his breath and looked towards the horizon. The sun was only a sliver in the sky. The pirates had chosen their time well. They soon would be battling in the dark when the attackers had the advantage. "Very well, my king. You have convinced me. But, if you get wounded, you are to go back to your cabin."

"Of course," Peter said. He'd prefer to fight alongside his comrades but he knew he should be grateful that Captain Sadon accepted him. He wouldn't press his luck.

"They're attacking, Captain!" Giles shouted from the top deck.

Sure enough, the intruder had come alongside the ship. Men from the enemy ship began pulling their vessel closer with ropes they'd attached to the ship with anchors. Simon came to stand by Peter's left and Rowan to the right. Each man drew his sword when Peter did and braced for the attack.

The enemy leapt onto the ship's landing and clashed with Captain Sadon's sailors. The air filled with the yells and screams of men. Peter recognized the cries of battle and charged forward with Simon and Rowan beside him.

Utter chaos ruled the ships as the battle raged on. Peter kept pushing the enemy back to their ship, ignoring the bleeding men around him. There would be time to help their own men and kill the injured pirates later. Now, he must focus on pushing his adversaries back. If not...a picture of Charlotte's face crossed his mind. Her fear-filled eyes met his and another surge of determination rushed through his veins. The enemy wouldn't defeat him so easily. Not when Charlotte's life lay on the line and these pirates stood in the way of reaching Myla.

He knocked another pirate to the ground and brought his sword against the man's head. The pirate collapsed and

Peter moved on to the next attacker. Bodies littered the ship's floor, making it difficult to walk without tripping. The dusk's dim lighting didn't benefit them either. Without the sun's light, it made it difficult to define friend from foe. A roar filled the air with the yells of the word 'smoke' and the remaining pirates all turned towards their craft.

Peter watched in confusion, not understanding the enemy's actions. Turning with them, he noticed a pillar of smoke rising above the pirates' ship.

The man who obviously assumed leadership started screaming orders for his men to retreat. The pirates followed the order and began clambering back onto their craft.

Giles and the rest of the sailors were swiping at them as they passed, making sure every single one was in his place.

"Peter!"

Simon ran up to him as the rest of the enemies filed into their craft and rowed away. The knight had a deep cut that ran across his cheek, but other than that, he came out unscathed. "We won, Peter! They're retreating!"

Peter smiled at the knight's enthusiasm. Pretty soon that excitement would die and he would harden like the rest of Peter's knights. A day he dreaded, for he didn't want Simon's personality to change. "Yes, Simon, I came to that conclusion seeing them retreat. You fought well."

"Thank you, Peter. I appreciate your compliment." Simon's eyes were shining with pride and Peter knew this victory meant a lot to him personally.

"The pirates are retreating at a quick pace," Giles informed, walking over to them. A slight limp to his left leg. "Some of my men went onboard while the enemy was distracted and reeked some havoc in the hold."

Peter didn't want to ask how much damage the sailors had done but Simon's curiosity voiced the subject anyway. "How? What did they do?"

"Let's just say they won't stay afloat for much longer," Giles replied nonchalantly. "They'll become part of the sea in a few minutes."

Peter simply nodded. "Will this delay our time sailing into Perdita?"

"No, my king. We will still dock on schedule."

That was a relief. Who knew how long Alice's herbs would hold out. Especially when Charlotte was still in death's clutches.

Chapter 11

Peter watched as Perdita's dock came into view, signaling their voyage's end. From a distance the docks looked empty except for one other ship. The port itself, unlike Cerulean's, was quiet and no people bustled around. Not even merchants and sailors hung about, carrying out their daily lives. The docks were in ruins as well. Not what Peter expected for another ocean town. Surely they would keep their port in working condition if they imported and exported goods? But, they were still at a distance. Perhaps when they drew closer the details would fill in.

"It's been a fine voyage, my king," Giles remarked, coming to stand alongside Peter.

Peter was about to mention the storm and attack from pirates to the first mate but bit his tongue. Giles had most likely experienced far worse storms and assaults than they had on this trip. Already out of his element, Peter dared not make a fool of himself by complaining about something these sailors considered normal. "If you say, Giles. I'll take your word for it."

Giles chuckled, seeming to catch Peter's uncertain tone. "My young king, when you live at sea from your first breath onward you experience many storms and roguish pirates. In time, it becomes normal and you learn to expect those things with every voyage."

Peter nodded, "I can understand that."

"Peter."

He turned at the familiar, but hoarse, voice.

Charlotte hobbled out, leaning on Alice for support. Behind them came the griffin who'd been locked in the hold until they docked.

Charlotte offered him a brave smile. Peter walked over to her just as she slipped from Alice's grasp and stumbled to him. He caught her by the elbows and gently pulled her to him. Peter saw Charlotte's face redden and he knew she was embarrassed for tripping in front of Giles and him. To distract her, he lead her to the railing. She cocked her head. "It's a quiet port," she said in a hoarse voice.

Peter grimaced at the sound. Even if she was up and walking, it did not hide the fact that she wasn't fully recovered yet. Only when her voice cleared, would he accept that she was well. "Yes, it is," he answered.

He let himself observe the port again although they weren't much closer. At a distance, the docks had looked empty and they still remained so. No people whatsoever were in sight. The store windows were shuttered and the merchants' stands were vacant. Strange. "Giles, are there not any people in Perdita?"

Giles looked at him as if he'd lost his mind. "Of course, my king. However, not many live here. Hence the name of the town."

Peter mused over that fact. Perdita did fit the town's current situation. Was it truly a 'lost city' as the name suggested? Due to the ruins covering the docks and the tattered storefronts, Peter had no problem believing it to be true.

The sailors tossed the anchor over the side and began throwing ropes to catch the posts, securing the ship to one of the docks.

"Well my king, I suppose this is farewell!"

Captain Sadon came up beside Giles, offering a bow to Charlotte. She nodded, but kept her mouth tight. Peter squeezed her hand, acknowledging her sore throat. "Yes, Captain, I suppose it is. I can't thank you enough for allowing us to travel with you. I will be forever grateful for your generosity."

Captain Sadon bowed again. "I am proud to escort our royals across the water. Whenever you need to sail back let me know and I will be honored to take you."

"Thank you, Captain."

Rowan, Simon, and Alice appeared behind Captain Sadon, each carrying a bag slung over their shoulders. Rowan nodded that they were ready to disembark.

"Captain, may I ask where we might find an apothecary?" Alice asked. "I must restock my herb supply."

"Yes, yes, my dear lady. You will find one only a block from here. They should have a sign that has a blue background and the image of a green leaf." Captain Sadon pointed to a road cutting through the town's buildings. "That street will lead you to the store, walk a bit further and you'll come to an inn."

"Thank you, Captain, for everything you have done for us." Alice smiled and turned to Charlotte. "I will restock on the fever and cough herbs that we need and see if they have anything for sore throats."

Charlotte only nodded that she heard and leaned against Peter. A new flash of concern and urge to move wakened inside him. Charlotte never leaned on anyone. She was a strong willed and independent woman who only recently began giving his advice any weight. Before that, she was as stubborn as an unmovable boulder.

Peter pressed his hand to the small of Charlotte's back and guided her off the rocking ship onto the dock. The land seemed to sway under him, making him stumble. But, he remained standing, fearing that he'd take Charlotte with him if he fell.

Giles chuckled. "You'll grow used to the land soon. Your feet just need to grow accustomed to the new ground."

Rowan helped Alice down and they experienced the same sensation. Simon disembarked only to stumble forward. His face immediately reddened and he gave Peter a sheepish smile before regaining his footing.

Crossing the empty street, Peter gestured for his small group to gather. "We need to make a plan. We need a strategy on how to talk to the town folk without setting off any alarms to the culprits who could be anywhere. But, first we need a place to rest and buy supplies."

Rowan put an arm around Alice's shoulder. "I'll help Alice get the herbs the queen needs."

"Very well, that works." He turned to Simon. "Did you by any chance ask the captain or Giles what currency we pay in here?"

"No, Peter. But I'm sure we can ask the people when they show up. Or the apothecary when we buy the herbs."

"Right, I guess that will have to do. Simon, I want you to search for a supply shop. That way we can stock up on food and other necessities."

Simon cocked his head. "If you don't mind me asking, Peter, why would we need food? We're staying at an inn, are we not?"

"I believe we'll attract less attention if we don't remain here. And, we won't draw unwanted attention from the bandits.

If we stay in the woods that lie on the outskirts, we'll be almost invisible."

"So I will be purchasing tents and camping supplies, then?" Simon asked.

"Yes, and don't buy too much. We need to remain as unnoticed as possible." Peter gestured for Simon's sword. "Give me your sword. That sheath will give away your status." Simon surrendered his blade and Peter gave him a bland dagger. "That shouldn't set anyone off, now will it?"

"No Peter. No one will look twice at me," Simon said, his face giving away his sullen mood since giving up his treasured weapon.

"Now, now. Don't act so childish," Peter said. "You'll have your sword back when you return." He turned to Rowan. "You may go with Alice to pick up the needed herbs. When you are finished, we shall meet up in the forest on the outskirts."

"Agreed, Peter." Rowan guided Alice away from the group and towards the apothecary. Simon took off trotting in the same direction.

Peter started to walk towards the tree line, his hand leading Charlotte, "Shall we?"

Charlotte made a feeble symbol for Luna and Ferox to follow her and proceeded to the forest ahead.

As they hurried to the trees' shelter, Peter prayed that Alice would find the right herbs and make it back soon. Charlotte was in grave danger and the fact that they were foreigners in a strange land didn't help in the matter at all.

Chapter 12

Alice skirted through the empty town with Rowan by her side. Walking through the streets, she'd hardly encountered any people. When they did, they did it with such a swift pace, Alice would have thought they were hiding from someone or something.

Alice felt Rowan's hand on the small of her back as he guided her to an old store front. Only then did she realize they'd reached their destination. The sign swinging on rusty hinges bore the remains of a faded image Alice could just make out to be a leaf.

She hurried over and entered through the open door. Shelves lined the back wall behind an ancient counter bearing more cracks than wood. The shelves against the wall were half empty and Alice's hopes for finding the correct herbs sank.

"Hello? Apothecary?" Rowan called.

"Yes, yes, I'm coming," a voice said from the back room. An elderly man with a beard of pure white drew aside the moth eaten curtain and hobbled out. He frowned, "Don't remember you two. You are foreigners, are ye not?"

"We are travelers looking for a stock of herbs," Rowan informed. "Do you by any chance have any..."

"Coriander," Alice blurted, "and horehound."

The old man nodded. "That I do. Ye having trouble with a coughing plague, eh?"

"Of a sort," Alice answered. "By the way, do you know of any other herbs that may help with coughing?"

The man turned from where he was sorting through the shelves. "I do not know too much. I am no physician like ye probably have, but a licorice and comfrey mixture fixes coughing up real good. Tried it on a few patients, that I did."

"I'll take that as well," Alice answered. "Who knows, perhaps a new mixture would do the trick."

The old man nodded and started going through another box on the shelf. After a few minutes, he set the herbs in separate piles on the counter.

Rowan pulled coins from his pocket. Frowning, he looked up at the apothecary. "What currency do you use here, apothecary?"

The old man snorted, "People 'round here take whatever they can get. Don't matter much as long as it's worth something."

"What do you prefer?"

"The good old fashioned Aurum coins will do. People as old as I am are still loyal to our king. King Philip's a wise ruler."

Alice almost gasped aloud. King Philip was long dead. Did news travel this slowly outside Aurum?

"I'm sorry, good man," Rowan started, "but Aurum's under new leadership now. King Philip passed on years ago."

The man's brow furrowed. "Is that so?" He huffed, "Who's sitting on the throne now?"

"Why his daughter, of course," Alice exclaimed. "Did you not hear of her coronation or perhaps her wedding?"

"Didn't even know his daughter existed," the apothecary replied. "We all thought she died a long time ago by that evil queen." He shook his head, "We don't get much news in these parts no more." He frowned, "You said she married? What lucky man holds the kingdom now? An earl? A prince?"

Alice tried not to laugh.

Rowan smiled and shook his head, "No, a baron. By the name of Lord Peter."

"A baron?" the man asked incredulously.

Rowan counted out a few gold coins and slipped them to the man. "Yes. The king's squire became a lord at a young age and then became king himself. And a wonderful king he has become."

"Well, I'll believe that when we don't have to live in fear of this emperor here," the man muttered.

Alice cocked her head, "What do you mean, kind sir?"

"Perdita used to belong to the kingdom of Aurum. But, the land was seized by a rogue lord many years ago when King Philip was a young man. The king lost the fight and retreated. We've been enslaved by the emperors that descended from the rogue lord ever since. We all live in fear that the present emperor will want to entertain his empress by sending the fire beast down upon our town."

"Fire beast?" Alice asked. Her hands started to shake as she gathered the herbs and dropped them into her sack.

"Yes, it's a beast I thought only existed in legends." The man's eyes portrayed a horror stricken expression. "But those monsters exist here. The emperor trains them to kill and set fire to poor villages. He slaughters people in his stadium with these beasts."

Alice stared at the man, horrified. Images of her own village on fire played through her mind. She never again wanted to experience another such event in her life.

"We should be going," Rowan said finally. He nodded to the man. "Thank you for your help, apothecary."

Alice let Rowan steer her towards the woods. The old man's words still swam in her head. *"Those monsters exist here…emperor trains them to kill…slaughters people in his stadium with these beasts."*

She tried to block the words from her mind. She needed to get this medicine to Charlotte and warn her about the fire beasts. If this place was that dangerous, they needed to find Myla, Gavin and Faye before it was too late.

The apothecary's words haunted Rowan from the moment he stepped out of the store. He was glad he'd stopped the man in the middle of his descriptive tales. The last thing he wanted was for Alice to wake up having nightmares. She'd had haunting dreams before about her village on fire and still suffered from them here and there. But this news could easily rouse them up into the full fledged, vivid nightmares of old. He wrapped his arm around her shoulder. He was her protector and felt so useless when she had those dreams. He could do nothing about it, except comfort her and tell her the dreams weren't real.

Another dreaded thought entered the front of his mind, it was about little Faye and Gavin, his precious children. Anger at himself surged to new life at the thought of what his children must be enduring. He scoffed in his mind, some protector he was. He couldn't even keep his own family safe! He shook his head. It was no use dwelling on his past faults. He needed to push forward. He needed to think about the future and help the king find the princess. His children would be wherever Myla was. The old man's words had given him an extra burst of energy and determination. Because, if what the man said was true, they were in more danger than they had realized.

———————————

Simon browsed the shelves of the local supply store. Peter had mentioned not to buy too much in order to avoid drawing unwanted attention. They were to be as invisible as possible. But how was he supposed to purchase everything they needed without looking suspicious? He sighed. He should have thought this through before entering the store.

He selected two rolls of hardy cloth that would serve as tents. He could endure sleeping outside while the others slept inside. The others needed shelter way more than he did. He thought back on what they'd brought in their trunks. Blankets, clothing…cookware? Was that necessary? It would be better to have too much than too little. He wandered over to the cooking utensils and started surveying the shelves with various pots.

The door burst open and three hooded men entered and walked straight to the counter. Simon shrank back to avoid being seen. The only person he wanted to know he was here was the shop owner.

The leader leaned over the counter and shouted towards the back, "Man, come here!"

The owner scurried over and eyed the men like a frightened mouse. "Yes?" he asked, trembling.

"The emperor's shipment was supposed to arrive today," the leader stated.

"Yes, I am aware of that fact," the owner replied, ringing his hands.

"Well," another man prompted. "Where is it, you fool?"

"It's not here yet…"

"What!" the leader shouted.

The owner flinched and Simon stepped farther back into the shadows.

"It's supposed to arrive soon," the owner managed.

The leader of the gang grabbed the man's collar. "Well, why haven't you moved your behind to go get it? The emperor is waiting for his beloved shipment to come in. There is something on board that is for his new princess."

Simon perked up at the word. Princess?

The leader tossed the owner aside and grunted, "No matter. We'll get it ourselves." The leader drew a dagger from beneath his cloak and waved it at the owner. "And it better be in prime condition or..." he rammed the dagger into the wooden counter, "I'll slit your sorry old throat."

Another one of the gang cocked his head and smirked. "Or better yet, perhaps we should send the fire beast."

At that the owner fell to his knees. "Gentlemen, I beseech ye! Do not send that monster! I'll do anything for the emperor! Just don't send that horrid beast, please!"

The three men let out a cacophonous laughter and strutted out the door.

Only when Simon heard their voices diminish did he come out of hiding. He grabbed the remaining things and walked up to the counter.

The owner still looked so shaken that Simon believed he didn't notice all the supplies Simon was purchasing. Slipping the man some money, Simon hoped the man didn't notice Aurum's emblem emblazoned on the coins.

"Princess?" he dared to ask.

"Yes, sir," the owner replied in a shaky voice. "The emperor has a new child. I don't know how, considering the empress is unable to have children. The child just appeared and no one dares question anyone further."

Dread rose in Simon's stomach at his rising conclusion. He had a feeling that he knew where that princess came from and who the rightful parents were.

Chapter 13

Peter woke when he felt Charlotte's warm body stir fitfully. Soon after arriving in the forest, she'd collapsed under a tree and had fallen into a deep sleep.

Looking down at her head resting on his chest, he pushed some stray hair from her face. Her skin felt like fire against his hand. Peter frowned and a new wave of worry crashed over him. He hoped Alice would come soon. Even with his little experience with medicine, his gut told him Charlotte was still in severe danger.

She released a moan, then sat straight up and began to let out harsh coughs. She covered her mouth with her hands and continued.

Peter rubbed her back gently. Her tenseness seemed to release with her coughs and she finally stopped.

Charlotte slipped her hands back down and her green eyes widened.

Peter took her hands in his and observed what she had seen. Blood pooled in miniature puddles in her palms while some of the liquid slipped down the palm of her hands and onto the ground.

"Charlotte…" Peter whispered.

She patted his shoulder with a weak hand and cracked a wan smile as if to reassure him that she'd be fine.

Luna, who'd been dozing nearby with Ferox, trotted up to her owner and smelled Charlotte's hands. The griffin's ears shot back and she let out a whine as she butted her owner's shoulder.

Charlotte smiled again and stroked Luna's coat, comforting the beast. Luna lay down at her feet and began to purr, which Peter thought sounded more like a growl. Charlotte opened her mouth and whispered. "Peter…I need…medicine."

"I know, Charlotte. Alice is buying more herbs as we speak. Soon you'll have your strength back." He grasped her hand, "Just hold on for a while longer."

Charlotte frowned. "But…Peter…" she protested.

"Shhh, now, love…" Peter soothed. "Don't wear your voice out talking to me. Rest for now."

She looked about to protest again but dropped her head on his shoulder and closed her eyes.

Alice walked into the clearing behind a thick brush and caught sight of Charlotte leaning on Peter's shoulder, sleeping. She smiled to herself at the sight. Charlotte wasn't one to publicly display affection towards her husband. But perhaps this sickness was teaching her to lean on others and not just herself.

Charlotte twitched, then began to cough. Peter turned her towards him immediately and held a red stained cloth to her mouth as more blood came from her mouth.

Alice raced across the clearing and dropped to her knees beside Charlotte. Peter looked at her with worried eyes, "Is she going to die?"

Alice looked at the king and saw real fear in his eyes. She'd never seen him reveal fear to anyone. He'd always kept it to himself. She didn't want to lie, but she also didn't want to give the king false hope. "I don't know, my king," she said. "We can only pray that she heals and that the medicine works."

Peter only nodded and tugged Charlotte closer to him.

Alice felt heartbroken. She'd watched Peter fall for Charlotte despite her sharp temper and attempts to ward off men. Charlotte had grown close to him as a friend and that relationship and trust had slowly become something more. In truth, she knew Charlotte was the one who needed to slowly trust him. Alice knew Peter was smitten with Charlotte ever since she saw them together when they brought Gavin home. She knew that if Charlotte didn't make it, the king would be torn.

Rowan knelt beside Peter and gave him a reassuring clap on the back. "Don't worry so, Peter. Your wife shall be fine."

Alice busied herself with unwrapping the herbs to avoid looking into Peter's gaze. She could tell he'd be able to read her doubts. She prayed the new herbs the apothecary recommended would do better than her other medicine.

After sorting out the herbs and gathering the ones she needed, she asked, "Is there a spring or a well you may have come by, Your Majesty?"

Peter looked up from Charlotte, "Yes, I heard some bubbling water nearby when I was coming here with the queen. It can't be far."

Rowan stood. "I'll search for it. You stay here with the queen, Alice." He trotted over to a bag they'd brought and took out a large cup. "How much water do you suppose you'll need?"

"Two of those cups will suffice," she said.

Rowan nodded and took off towards the trees.

Simon emerged from the trees, trailing two horses behind him that carried all the supplies he'd purchased. He immediately saw Peter leaning against an old oak tree with the queen resting by his side. Alice was crushing some leaves and mixing them in water, while the two griffins slept right near the queen's feet.

"Simon." Peter flicked his wrist to Luna and gestured for the beast to take his spot. Luna obliged and curled up next to the queen, allowing her to lean into the griffin's black fur.

Peter approached Simon and drew him away from the women. "Did you find everything?"

Simon gestured to the horses. "All the supplies are in the sacks these animals are carrying. I only bought two horses for fear of being noticed."

Peter nodded, "That's good. No one noticed you, then?"

Simon shook his head, "No, Peter. The people didn't seem at all curious about why I was purchasing all these supplies. But, there is one thing I must mention."

"Simon, I see you were successful." Rowan broke through the brush to the left and walked over to join them.

"Yes, he was," Peter said, "but, I'm afraid he has something more to tell us."

Rowan cocked his head in interest. "Go on."

"While I was buying all our supplies three men came into the store. They were rather suspicious looking so I hid in the shadows, not wanting to announce my presence."

Peter nodded his appreciation.

"They walked straight up to the counter and demanded the owner to give them the shipment that had arrived today. The leader of this group was especially cruel and I was grateful that I was hidden. But, what really caught my attention was a comment the leader made."

"What would that be?" Peter asked.

"He said the emperor of this land needed the shipment because it held an important object for his new princess."

Peter perked at the word. "Princess you say?"

"Yes, Peter. At first I wasn't the least bit interested but then I started to put the pieces together. When I purchased the supplies, I dared to ask who the princess was. The owner didn't reveal any names, and he didn't seem to know where she had come from. He said the empress had never been able to have children. But an heir suddenly appeared."

Simon watched Peter's expression. His eyes widened, then narrowed. "You are suggesting that this princess is really my daughter?"

"Yes, Peter."

Peter exchanged a glance with Rowan. The steward had remained silent through the whole exchange and simply listened. But Simon could tell his hopes of finding his children were as high as Peter's.

"I believe you may be onto something, Simon," Peter said. "Well done."

"Thank you, Peter," Simon replied, "but, there is one more matter."

"Which is?"

"We are too close to the town," Simon began. "I believe we'll have to move deeper into these woods. I don't think it's safe to be this close to Perdita. If ever some of the emperor's men find us there's no telling what they'll do. I heard tell of a fire beast that destroys everything in its path."

"I heard of that creature from the apothecary as well," Rowan added. "He said it burned whole villages down and is trained to kill."

Peter's eyes widened. "Then I take it we will move deeper into the forest where we will not be disturbed. If this emperor has my daughter I'll have to find a way to get her. The farther away we are from civilization, the less people know we're here, giving us more time to consider our next move."

Chapter 14

Charlotte took the cup from Alice's outstretched hand and smelled the herbal tea Alice had prepared.

"It's a new formula the apothecary recommended for coughs," Alice remarked. "It's a mixture of…"

"Licorice and comfrey," Charlotte managed to whisper.

Alice gaped. "Why yes! That's exactly what it is!" She frowned and put a hand to her chin. "But how did you know? I never used such a mixture before."

"Your mother had much more to teach us, Alice," Charlotte answered. A cough rose in her throat, making her hack it out. Her throat burned in outrage at her attempt to get rid of the cough. Charlotte put the cup to her lips and let the warm liquid run down her sore throat, soothing it.

She laid against her pillows in the interior of her tent and gazed out the tent flaps. Peter had moved the entire camp further into the woods that afternoon and wouldn't give an explanation when she asked. He simply said he'd tell her later and ordered her to ride on one of the horses or Luna.

Now the second camp was set up with the supplies Simon had purchased which included two tents, one for Charlotte and Peter and the other for Rowan and Alice. The horses grazed in the woods tied to trees and the griffins lay in the shade by their tents.

An evening breeze swept the tent flaps up and entered the warm tent. Charlotte closed her eyes and let the cool breeze wash over her. She hummed in her throat and leaned back again.

She gave the cup back to Alice, who was content just to remain by her side in a peaceful silence. Charlotte let her thoughts wander with the breeze. Despite Peter's best attempts to keep quiet about the sudden moving, she had overheard Simon mentioning Myla and a group of ruffians. Her guess was that Peter wanted to protect them and that the men had some link to Myla. Hopefully Peter would have some sense and come tell her soon.

"Charlotte."

Her eyes flew open at the sound of his voice. As if summoned, Peter stood near the outside of the tent, leaning against the frame. "May I come in?"

She nodded, not wanting to use her voice until she needed it most. She might be able to speak, but only short sentences full of pain.

Alice looked at Charlotte then at Peter, who'd remained at the frame. She shot Charlotte a honeyed smile. "I'll leave you two alone." With that, Alice jumped from her seat and hurried out before Charlotte could protest.

She frowned after Alice. Her friend was always making up excuses for leaving Peter alone with her. She knew Alice meant well, but Charlotte still grew nervous around him. Even being married to him for two years hadn't changed much. When he was just her friend, it was different.

Peter entered and smiled down at her. "How are you feeling? Alice said she gave you a different type of medicine."

"Yes, she did. And I'm not so bad anymore."

"That's a lie," Peter remarked matter-of-factly, sitting down next to her. "I can hear the harshness in your voice."

Charlotte gulped and shot him a searing glare. "Fine."

Peter let out a chuckle and leaned against the pillows and opened his arms to her.

When she hesitated he gazed at her with a wounded look. "Charlotte, come here."

Under his hurt blue eyes she gave up and leaned into him. A little cough escaped her as she felt his warm arms wrap around her. She let her heart rule over this one and snuggled into him. "Are you going to tell me why we moved camp?" she asked in a whisper.

Peter sighed. "If you insist. After all, I did promise to tell you later."

She listened without interrupting while Peter told her about Simon's discovery. He also told her what Rowan and Alice had heard in the apothecary's shop. "So you believe the emperor has Myla?" she asked after he finished.

"Yes, I do."

"And Perdita really used to be under our dominion?"

"Correct again," Peter answered. "Perhaps after we get Myla back I'll wage war and earn the land back. It would be for King Philip, he was the one who lost it. I would earn it back for him."

"Maybe," was all Charlotte said.

"Pardon?"

"I don't feel comfortable letting you go off to war," she said. Then, adding to make sure he didn't think she was selfish, "I would like Myla to have a father to raise her."

"Oh?" He wrapped his arms tighter around her, let out a laugh, and teased, "You would miss me as well, would you not?"

She felt her cheeks redden. "Perhaps, perhaps not," she managed. Another cough rose in her throat out of nowhere and she let it out. She winced when she saw the red spots on Peter's doublet. Even with the garment's dark coloring, the blood was still visible up close.

Peter didn't seem to care about the piece of clothing. Instead, he cupped her cheeks. "I'm wearing you out with my talking, Charlotte. You should rest."

"I'm not tired," she said. Her throat burned but she didn't want to admit it.

He grasped her chin and frowned at her. "Don't try to fool me, Charlotte."

"I'm not."

"Yes, I believe you are." He gestured to the sinking sun. "It's past time you went to bed, anyway. With your sickness, Alice repeatedly said you should rest."

"I know that," she snapped, regretting it in the end. Her throat protested with screaming pain.

Peter must have seen her wince. "Oh yes, you know what she said. However, you're not following her instructions." He sat up and carefully laid her head on the soft pillows. Then, leaning over he pressed a soft kiss to her forehead. "Sleep well, Charlotte."

Darkness surrounded Simon on both sides. The moon was a thin sliver in the black sky. He could barely make out the shadows of the trees that engulfed them on all sides. He feared that if an enemy crept up on them, he wouldn't be able to see and it would be too late.

When Peter announced that they'd be taking shifts guarding the camp, Simon had agreed to take the first watch.

But, considering the night's blackness, he was reconsidering his offer.

A twig cracked behind him and he whirled around, hand on his sheath.

An outline of a man stood before him.

"Who goes there?" he demanded.

The man held up his hands, "Simon, it's me, Rowan."

Simon let his shoulders roll back. "Oh, Rowan. You frightened me. I'm glad it is only you. I feared it was our enemies."

Rowan shook his head. "I don't believe the enemy will ever discover us here. We are safe for the most part."

"You should try to tell Peter that," Simon said.

"Now, now, calm down. The king is only concerned about our safety, especially the women's. He is only taking precautions."

"I guess so."

Rowan clapped him on the shoulder. "When you're ready to sleep, let me know and I'll take the next shift."

"Will do."

Rowan started to walk off when he turned again, "And Simon?"

"Yes?"

"I never did thank you for letting Alice and I have the remaining tent. That was very thoughtful of you."

Simon shrugged. "Your welcome. I'm a lone person and don't need that much space and I thought the tent would offer your wife more security."

"Thank you again." Rowan walked back to the site and slipped into the tent across from Peter's.

Luna perked up when Rowan passed, but laid back down when she saw it was only him. Simon smiled at the beast's protective nature. Since the queen had brought the griffins back to her castle, he'd grown used to them and respected them for their loyalty to Queen Charlotte.

A rustle in the bushes made him whip around towards the woods. He peered into the trees, but caught sight of nothing. An uneasy feeling filled his stomach and he found his gaze settled on a particular clump of brambles. Even though he didn't hear any more noises and saw nothing out of the ordinary, he couldn't shake the feeling that something was out there.

A growl sounded behind him and he noticed Luna and Ferox were standing up, hackles raised. Something had startled them. But what? Ferox let out a hiss and kept staring in the direction of the brambles Simon was peering into.

Then, he saw it. A shadow slinked across the forest floor like a ghost, not making a sound. His hand went to the weapon at his side. The trees' branches swayed, casting more shadows across the landscape. Perhaps the shadow was simply a branch?

There was only one way to find out. Follow it.

He made his way into the woods towards the brush. Luna and Ferox were pacing around the campsite now, eyes on the bush near him. He drew his sword and felt himself relax with the weapon in his hand. Taking a deep, silent breath, he continued towards the bushes.

Once he got near enough, he leapt behind the bush and hacked at the brambles with his blade. Nothing. He straightened and surveyed his surroundings, not wanting to take a chance on someone or something attacking him. Nothing seemed out of the ordinary. The trees' branches swayed to and fro in the night breeze, and clouds swept across the sky, covering the moon. Without the only light in the sky, the woods seemed to grow darker.

Silence reigned superior as Simon kept looking from left to right, scouring the land. The silence was the only thing that didn't settle well with him. No bird nor night scavenger stirred. It was too quiet. Just a little too peaceful.

Behind him he could hear Luna and Ferox growling in the distance. After another quick survey, he headed back to the camp.

A rustle of leaves sounded behind him. He whirled around, sword still in hand. A hard object struck him on the forehead. He felt his knees grow weak as he tried to fight consciousness. Just before his world went black, he felt the cold, sharp edge of a blade against his neck.

———————

Peter's eyes flew open. A feeling of unease made its way up his body. Something wasn't right. He could hear the griffins growling softly outside. He sat up and strained his ears for any unfamiliar sound in the night. Except for the griffins' growls, he could hear nothing alarming. But that was exactly the point. The night was just a little too quiet. Simon was out there, but hadn't come to warn him of any danger.

He checked to make sure his sword was in reach and that a dagger was near Charlotte. He didn't want to leave her defenseless if this turned out to be an ambush. He crept to the tent's doorway and peered out. Luna and Ferox both had their hackles raised as they pranced around the campsite, eyes on the woods. He frowned. From his view, nothing seemed out of place. But, something had alarmed the beasts and whatever was out there wasn't leaving. And where was Simon? He was supposed to be keeping watch by the trees.

Peter made his way back to his pallet next to Charlotte and grabbed his sword. Perhaps if he went outside he'd see better. If something wasn't right, he'd warn Rowan.

"Peter?"

He looked down to see Charlotte squinting up at him. Her eyes were dull, but he knew he had her full attention.

"What's wrong?" she asked, looking from him to the weapon in his hands.

"Hopefully nothing," he replied. "I'm just going to have a look around and see if Simon needs help."

"Is he in trouble?"

"I can't answer that either," he said. He pressed the dagger into her weak palm. "If anything comes, use that."

She nodded and sat up.

Peter slipped back over to the tent flaps and lifted one up. He crept out and stood, peering into the night. Luna came over to him and gave him a good whiff before calming down. "What do you see, Luna?" Peter asked in a whisper.

As if in an answer, she looked back to where Simon was supposed to be watching. He signaled for Luna to stand by their tent, guarding Charlotte, while he walked on silent feet over to where Simon had stood.

He took in his surroundings, noting the footprints leading farther into the woods. Glancing around, he followed them. The prints led him to a large pile of brambles and a bush. After that, they seemed to rear back towards camp. He glanced around him once more before turning back the way he had come. His eye caught something in the soil. He stooped down to get a closer look and drew in a breath. The footprints turned into a mash of unidentified lines. Whoever the prints belonged to had a struggle and was dragged away.

Peter stood up and did another quick survey. How long had Simon been gone?

Just when he was about to follow the disturbed prints, a scream echoed through the night.

He charged back through the trees and halted mid step at the scene in front of him. At least a dozen men in the darkest clothes Peter had ever seen were attacking the camp with fire. Alice's screams could be heard from Rowan and her tent. Ferox was in front of the their tent, hissing at the men who dared to come close. Luna was where Peter had ordered her to stay, next to his own tent.

Luna lashed out with her long talons, striking the man nearest to her. The man cried out in agony and dropped to the ground. Peter didn't have to be up close to see the blood gushing from the man's side.

He melted into the shadows. As long as he stayed in the trees the men couldn't see him. He began to creep to the backside of Rowan's tent. If he could get to the tent, he'd be able to take the enemy by surprise.

The men had already tied up their horses and were raiding their sacks of belongings. Still Peter kept heading for Rowan's tent. Alice let out another blood curdling scream worse than the last. To his horror, the men had somehow managed to tie Ferox's muzzle shut and had roped it to the ground. To Peter's relief, Luna was still standing and sending any man near her to the ground with a huge gash.

He finished his journey to Rowan's tent and assessed the situation. The men had entered the tent and he could hear Rowan's grunts of combat and Alice's screams.

Drawing closer, Peter waited behind a tree for his moment to enter the fight. When the men stumbled out of the tent and had their backs turned from him, he leapt from the shadows, striking the first man he saw. He worked on stabbing another one, when Rowan's head popped out along with Alice's frantic face.

"Stay in the tent, dear," Rowan ordered. With that, he joined in and starting attacking the man nearest to him.

Luna's yowl pierced the air and Peter turned to see the black griffin stumble and one of the men take advantage and enter the tent. Luna screeched her protest and went after the man. Seeing Rowan taking down most of the men, Peter charged over.

Shoving off the remaining men and letting Luna take care of the rest of them, Peter opened the tent. Charlotte was wide-eyed, her green gaze piercing the man beside her. Anger boiled in Peter at the sight of another man near Charlotte. He came over to her side and wrapped a protective arm around her middle. Raising his sword, he prepared to run the man through.

Charlotte touched his arm with her weak hand and gestured to the man's tunic. It was wet, and blood spilled out from the wound, staining the sheets red. There was no doubt. The man was dead.

The dagger in Charlotte's hand was dripping with blood like she'd driven the blade in several times. "He's dead, Peter," she said weakly.

He allowed himself to relax for a moment and soak in the fact that the woman he loved was safe. He pulled her against him, hugged her and pressed a quick kiss to her temple.

All of a sudden, her shoulders grew tense and he heard her whisper, "Peter." But the whisper wasn't one of content; it was one of fear.

He turned around, only to feel cold metal ram into his head. With that, darkness won.

Chapter 15

Something wet hit Peter's face, making him jolt awake. He groaned and sat up, blinking away his sleep. He looked around him in confusion. He was in a small, dark room with thick bars. The sudden realization hit him that he was in a cell. But where was he? In a cell where?

He shot up from his seated position, only to sit back down as excruciating pain filled his head. Peter put his head in his hands and waited for the pain to subside. However, with the pain, came the earlier memories of Simon missing, the ambush, and himself being knocked unconscious.

Raising his head, he took his time surveying his surroundings. Because of the darkness, he couldn't see much but the stone walls and the bars. He felt moss beneath his fingers that was growing on the cold floor and heard the ever present dripping of water from the upper level.

Then, he realized he was alone. Just one feeble person in a dark dungeon. Where were the others? Was this the place where Simon was brought to? What about Rowan and Alice? And Charlotte? Dread filled him at the memory of her. The last time he'd seen her was when she was in his arms, protecting her from the ambushers. His worry for her rose as he wondered what the ruffians had done to her when they'd knocked him unconscious. He prayed that the griffins had been able to protect her.

A clanging of metal made him look out into the hall. A guard bearing a torch walked towards him. Peter hurried to the cell's door, clasped the bars, and raised his voice, "Guard, where am I?"

The guard turned towards him and laughed in mockery, "Oh it is His Majesty."

"Enough! Where am I? I demand an answer."

"You're the great emperor's guest, King Peter," the guard answered.

Peter frowned, "How do you know I am a king?"

"Oh, we know more than we let on, King Peter. The high officials of Perdita know way more than the peasants do. When the emperor got wind that you were looking for your missing princess and that you were here, you and your company were a threat. So, he released his men to ambush you."

"So you have the others? Where are they? Especially the queen?"

The guard only laughed. "You will see in time."

"What have you done with my wife!" Peter demanded, his anger growing with every word.

"In time you will see her. At least that is what I've been told. Perhaps you will, perhaps you will not. It all depends on how gracious the emperor is feeling."

Peter threw another question at the man, willing him to keep talking. If he could pry enough information from him, he could build a slight understanding on what had happened. "How did your emperor know we came?"

"Again, that will be revealed in time." The guard spun on his heel and started back down the hall.

Peter called after him but the man ignored him. He groaned and sank to the floor, not caring that he was right under a drip in the ceiling. He put his head to his knees and closed his eyes. He didn't care what they did to him, he just wanted to know that his company was safe, especially Charlotte and Myla. He felt sleep call him and he allowed it to sweep over him.

———————

He woke to the sound of the metal door creaking upon its hinges. Peter sat up and squinted out into the hall. His head ached with his quick jerk, and he put his hands against his temples, gritting his teeth at the pain.

The guard appeared from down the hall, dragging a figure after him. Only when they got closer did the figure become recognizable. "Charlotte," he uttered under his breath.

The guard came to the front of his cell and started unlocking the metal door. Peter observed Charlotte with horror. Her dress was soiled and marked with drops of blood, Peter guessed was from her coughing. Her eyes mirrored a dullness Peter wasn't used to seeing. Her head drooped and her knees seemed to give way beneath her.

The guard growled and yanked her back up straight.

"How dare you!" Peter shouted, jumping to his feet. His rage began to boil up again and he knew it wouldn't be the last time his temper flared with the man.

"Peter…"

He flicked his attention back to Charlotte. Hearing him shout must have brought her back to the present situation. She was looking at him with a curious gaze, as if uncertain he was really there.

"Yes, love. It's me," he soothed.

"Shut up, king," the guard snapped, "save your sweetened words for later."

"What are you planning to do with my queen?" Peter demanded.

Without answering, the guard swung the door open and shoved Charlotte into the cell.

Peter caught her just before she fell onto the stone floor.

"Getting her out of the way," the guard finally said. "She's been nothing but trouble. Maybe with you she'll have some sense to behave."

Peter looked at Charlotte leaning against his chest, shaking. "Surely she was no trouble?" he dared to voice. "She's shaken and is as weak as a newborn lamb."

The guard scoffed, "We tried to get her to eat, but she won't, that's why she's weak. The emperor wants her and you alive for a special presentation before you die." He pointed a finger at Charlotte. "With her not eating she's disobeying the emperor. If she doesn't eat and show anything but skin and bones, my men will beat her into submission."

Peter wrapped his arms around her and moved her so that his body protected her from this beast. "You will do no such thing while I'm still alive!" he said fiercely. "You will not harm her, do you hear?"

"Oh I hear all right, o high and mighty," the guard mocked. "Just make sure she eats. The emperor wants you weak but still alive."

"She won't eat because she's sick," Peter said. "I need medicine to get her to eat."

The guard cocked his head as if showing interest. "Is that so? How sick is she?"

"She's coughing up blood," Peter said, "do I really need to expound on that fact?"

The guard shook his head and didn't speak.

Peter took advantage of the pause and asked the question that had nagged his mind since waking up in prison. "Who brought us here?"

The guard laughed. "I told you before. All will be revealed in time." With that he rammed the cell door closed, making Peter's head ring. "Now, shut your mouth, and comfort your precious queen."

"What about the medicine?" Peter asked.

"King, we only want you alive for a few days. The sicker she is, the better." With that, he stalked off.

Peter watched the man leave, slamming the door behind him. Charlotte coughed in his arms and he looked down at her again. He felt her knees grow weak and before she collapsed, he picked her up, cradling her in his arms. Her light frame made his worry rise even more. He could feel her bones beneath her skin and knew the guard's claim was true.

She looked up at him and murmured something he didn't catch.

Peter walked to the back of the cell to a dry place on the floor and lowered himself to the ground still holding her. He shifted to his side and laid her gently on the floor.

Charlotte leaned against the wall and glanced at him with dull eyes. Even though they seemed to be vacant, she still managed to pass a question through her gaze. What was he doing?

As an answer, he took off his doublet, flipped it inside out, and bundled it into a makeshift pillow. He put the creation next to him on the floor and nodded for her to put her head down. She cracked a smile of appreciation and scooted down to the doublet and laid her head on it. She touched his shoulder, "Thank you...Peter," she whispered.

"You're worth it," he answered. "Now, don't make your throat sore talking to me. Rest, love."

She consented to his request, turned on her side, and closed her eyes.

Peter couldn't tell how many hours had passed or what time it was because of the darkness. Neither the cell nor the hall had any windows, leaving one to guess how many hours had passed. The only light came from a dim torch hung on the wall outside the cell. A whole day could have gone by and he wouldn't have known. He could only guess it was near midnight due to the unusual quietness in the distance. There used to be at least the sound of bustling servants and a strange roaring sound coming from, what sounded like another building.

Charlotte was still asleep by his side, woken only by the ever present coughing.

Peter looked up at the sound of the creaking door expecting to see the guard. Instead, a young boy followed by a soldier with a torch entered. Before the boy could get too far, the soldier grabbed his shirt and yanked him back. The force made the boy's feet leave the floor and he scrambled for a grip when the soldier dropped him. The man leaned down to meet the boy's eyes and began talking to him in a harsh whisper.

The boy seemed to be around seven and kept his head bowed when the soldier spoke to him. Was it a sign of respect or fear? Peter would guarantee it was a show of fear. He'd only docked in Perdita a short time ago and he already knew the land was barbarous.

The soldier straightened and thrust the torch at the boy, making the lad leap back. The soldier growled something and thrust it towards the child again. Out of obedient reluctance, the boy grabbed the torch and began to walk towards Peter.

The soldier walked close behind until a yell echoed from across the hall and the soldier shoved the boy aside and ran to meet a shadow on the other end.

The lad stumbled and nearly burned himself in the act. When he drew nearer, Peter noticed the child to be Gavin. Rowan's son was dressed in a tattered tan tunic. His skin was smudged with dirt and grit from hard labor and tear streaks were freshly formed on his ruddy cheeks.

As Gavin pattered by, Peter took advantage and waved his hands. "Gavin!"

Gavin's head whirled around and his eyes widened. "King Peter!" He looked towards the soldier and the shadow before coming over to the cell. "Yes, my king?"

Peter nodded to the soldier and whispered to him, "Are you allowed to speak with me?"

"No, my master has forbidden me to."

"Then I will make this quick," Peter answered, keeping an eye on the soldier. "I need your help."

"How, my king?"

"I need you to go into town and get herbs for Queen Charlotte and then smuggle them to me when you walk this way again."

"My king!" Gavin gasped. "How can I do that?"

"You must find a way!" Peter said fiercely. "Aurum's future hangs on a weak thread. The queen is growing weaker by the hour and I don't have the slightest idea where my daughter is."

Gavin leaned forward, "My king, I think I may know."

Peter reached through the bars and clasped Gavin's thin arm. "You know where she is?"

"I can guess. I have heard her crying when I carry out my orders."

Peter's heart sank. "So you don't know exactly where she is?"

Gavin hung his head. "No, my king. My guess is that she is being kept with the older women who are assigned to handle the empress' children. Except the empress has no other children except for the princess."

Peter blew out a breath. At least he knew Myla wasn't in any sort of danger. She had women taking care of her because she was meant to be the emperor and empress' child. His anger rose. How dare they take his child! How dare they steal Aurum's heir!

His anger subsided when Gavin looked up at him shyly and asked. "If I may, my king, where are my parents? I can't find them."

Peter was the one now to hang his head. "I don't know, Gavin. We were separated when we were brought here."

Disappointment covered the boy's face. "Oh."

Peter shook the boy's arm gently through the bars. "That is why you must help me smuggle medicine to the queen. If she gets stronger, I'll be able to help your family. And you'll help mine and the kingdom."

Gavin nodded and stood up taller. "All right, my king. I will try. What herbs am I to look for?"

"You're looking for something by the name of licorice and comfrey. Do you know where the apothecary is?" At Gavin's nod he continued, "Just ask him for those herbs and he'll find them for you."

Gavin nodded again, "Licorice and comfrey."

"Yes, now go before your master sees you talking to me."

Gavin glanced around and then hurried away down the hall, taking the only light with him.

Blood filled her mouth. Charlotte sat up and wretched the putrid tasting liquid out. She hated it. Hated the sickness for entering her body and hated herself for not talking about the proper medicine to use. Now they were prisoners and no hope of a cure seemed within reach. The last time she'd seen Alice was when her friend had tried to give her medicine and the guard dragged her to Peter's cell. He must have thought she'd grow weaker without the help of Alice's herb supply. Little did he know that she possessed the knowledge of an herb that could cure her completely.

She watched Peter approach her after looking out of the bars. She'd woken up when he was conversing with someone, but couldn't define what they were speaking of. She'd just fallen back to sleep.

Peter lowered himself to the ground beside her in his usual spot and looked down at her with worried eyes. She smiled to reassure him and patted his arm. Her throat still ached from her coughing attack and she dared not speak. Not yet.

Chapter 16

Nothing happened. Peter waited for seemingly endless days and nights for Gavin's return with the herbs, but the boy still hadn't come. Not knowing whether it was day or night didn't help the matter. The waiting only dragged on longer. Every day was the same. The guard would bring them their portion of food for the day and a cup of water; just enough to keep them breathing.

Charlotte refused to touch any of the food. When Peter offered her a portion, she looked at it with disgust and refused. "Charlotte, you must eat," Peter told her one morning. "You're getting too weak and have to give your body energy."

"I can't, Peter," she replied, her voice sounding no better than the other day. "I'm not hungry, I can't bear to touch that food."

Peter's anxiety grew as he watched Charlotte start to fade before his eyes. The coughing had grown worse with each passing hour. Her frame was skin and bones and her eyes vacant and dull. The only reassurance of her being alive was her breathing and when she spoke with him in short phrases.

As the hours dragged by with no sign of Gavin, Peter began to worry that the boy had gotten caught speaking with him and that his master wouldn't let him roam by himself. If that was the case, Peter knew there was no hope for Charlotte.

He fell against the wall next to her sleeping form many hours later and took her hand in his. It was warm; but just barely. "Oh, Lord, please," Peter whispered to the ceiling.

A patter of running feet came his way, making him look towards the cell door. "My king?" came a small voice.

Gavin.

Peter leapt up, careful not to wake Charlotte, and ran to the door. "Gavin, oh mercy it's good to see you! Have you got the herbs?"

Gavin's face fell. "My king, I was unable to sneak away. My master watched me nonstop."

Peter's hopes sank. "So you don't have the herbs?" He tried to hide his disappointment and not dwell on what that might mean for Charlotte. He failed miserably, for Gavin must have read it on his face.

"I found my parents, my king," Gavin announced, bouncing slightly. "They are not far from your cell, just through that door down the hall," he said, pointing towards the long hall Gavin's master had walked to.

Peter tried to crack a smile, "That's wonderful, Gavin."

Gavin held his hands behind his back and Peter thought nothing of it. That was until the boy brought out a mug filled with a liquid smelling of a flavor Peter thought he recognized. "This is for the queen," Gavin informed. "My mother told me to find a way to give it to the queen. Thank the Lord I knew where to find you."

The mug was just slim enough to pass through the cell's bars. Peter took the mug from Gavin's thin hand and smiled. "Thank you, Gavin. You don't know how much hope this has brought me today."

Gavin cocked his head and asked, "Is Queen Charlotte going to die?"

His innocent question rocked Peter's foundation. He'd been asking himself the same question over and over again. Peter battled with his emotions, struggling to come up with an answer that wouldn't reveal his fear. But it was pointless. His voice sounded haunted with every word he uttered. "I don't know, Gavin. She's very weak."

Gavin nodded to the cup. "Perhaps the medicine will help. I know it's cold but my mother says it shall work the same way as if it was warm."

Peter nodded. "Yes, we will see. You're a good boy, Gavin. Now go before someone sees you. I don't know when your master will call for you."

Gavin stepped back. "He had an assignment given to him by the emperor and he left me here. Whenever I have a chance I will see if my mother has more herbs from her bag and if she has another cup ready."

Peter smiled. Perhaps there was hope on the horizon now. "That would be a miracle and a prayer answered." He frowned, "But, how does your mother still have her herbs?"

"The guards searched my father for weapons thoroughly. My mother was able to hide the herbs in her clothing. When they didn't find any weapons on her, they were satisfied. They never guessed she was hiding the medicine designed to make the queen well."

Peter nodded then jerked his head towards the hall. "Gavin, you must leave now. I don't want you getting caught."

With that the boy was gone, running towards the hall and out of Peter's life for the moment.

Peter made his way back to Charlotte's side and sank to the floor. He touched her shoulder and shook her gently. "Charlotte, wake up, please. I have something for you."

She squinted up at him through sleep-filled eyes. "What is it, Peter?"

He showed her the cup. "Gavin brought this medicine for you to take. Your coughing will finally stop."

She gave no answer, just sat up and took the cup with shaking hands. She tilted it back and drank the liquid. Giving the cup back to Peter, she scrunched her nose up and said, "It tastes awful."

Peter shook the cup to make sure she got every drop. She had. "It will make you well though," he said. "You'll grow stronger."

She laid back down and shut her eyes. Peter thought she was asleep until he heard the words. "Perhaps, Peter, perhaps."

───────────

Dark shadows crowded around Charlotte. She stood in an open arena surrounded by shadowy figures. They all whispered the same thing. In a chant that made chills roll over her. "You will die. You will die. You will die," they taunted in an evil voice.

She watched as the shadows lifted, but hung over her like the voices. A cloud of smoke, darker than night flooded the arena and came towards her. The voices continued to chant, "You will die. You will die…"

Flames sparked from the smoke's interior. Hot tongues of fire started towards her, hissing their intentions in the chilling chant of the shadowy figures. "You will die. You will die."

Charlotte felt the hot flames start to lick her clothing and she cried out. She was defenseless against the hungry fire. It had one purpose, to devour her. She cried out again as the fire licked her skin. Searing pain shot up her body. Tears sprang to her eyes as she cried again.

A soft voice called out to her. "Charlotte...lungwort... Charlotte...lungwort."

The fire continued to eat at her clothing.

The evil chant continued, "You will die..."

But the soft calling shouted above the hated words, "Charlotte...lungwort."

She finally realized what the voice was trying to tell her. She nodded and shouted to the shadows. "You will not defeat me! I will rise again!"

Laughter echoed around her. And the voices continued their chant, "You will die..."

Fire scorched her skin, making her scream in terror. The soft voice grew louder still, "Charlotte...Charlotte..."

Peter brushed Charlotte's shoulder and whispered softly to her, "Charlotte...wake up, love."

She jerked again and let out another screech. Peter knew it to be one of her nightmares. She suffered from them every once in a while. They always were the same; about her village on fire.

"Charlotte..."

This time she responded. She sat up and looked around her, shaking. Her breathing was rapid and she jerked from side to side.

Peter ran a hand up her arm. "Charlotte...are you...?"

She shot away from him and screeched. Even though it was dark Peter knew terror was in her eyes. It was always in her gaze when the nightmare ended. He whispered softly again, "Charlotte, it's me, Peter."

She finally seemed to realize who he was, for her breathing relaxed.

"Are you all right, love?" he asked, rubbing her shoulder.

"I'm fine now that I'm awake," she replied, still taking deep breaths.

"It was a nightmare about the fire wasn't it?"

She shook her head, surprising Peter. "No, no it wasn't. Well, about a different fire." She took a deep breath and gripped his hand. "There were voices taunting me and telling me I was going to die. Another voice was calling out and saying..." her grip hardened and she yanked at his arm. He winced at the surprising strength she still held. "Peter you need to find me medicine."

"Gavin will return with more..."

"No, a different herb. It cures the sickness I have completely. Alice does not know of the illness I have. She only knows how to treat me with cough herbs."

She gripped his skin tighter. Peter felt sure that his skin would be red where her hand was. He loosened her hand and held it. "Charlotte, why didn't you tell me this before?"

"I never could." Her voice started to crack. "My throat would scream at me whenever I tried." She broke off coughing. Harsh, liquid-sounding coughs, wracking her weak body. Peter heard her clear her moist throat and whisper, "I need lungwort. That is the name of the herb, lungwort. You must find a way to get it."

She laid back down. "Have Alice make a drink out of the herb and give it to me. I need it or else..." she faded.

He continued to hold her hand, "Or else?" He knew what she was going to say but wanted to hear it from her lips first. He could only believe it then.

"Or else...I'll die."

Chapter 17

The hours passed in foreboding agony. Peter waited for Gavin to return, but saw no sign of him. Charlotte reminded him of the urgent need to find lungwort and Peter could only tell her to cling to life a little longer.

One morning the guard brought Peter the daily food and watched him eat. "Make that queen eat," he ordered.

"I beg your pardon?"

"I want to see that she's eating," the guard said. She seems to be growing weaker. If she dies, the emperor will not be happy."

"I can't force her to eat," Peter replied.

The guard reached for the keys in his pocket. "Then I'll get her to eat. Even if I have to force it down her throat."

Peter slid towards Charlotte's form. Her body was trembling but her eyes burned like fire into the guards'. "You will do no such thing," Peter said. He blocked the guard's path with his own body. "You will have to kill me to get to her. I don't believe the emperor will be pleased to hear that you killed one of his captors without permission."

The man scowled at him, obviously upset that Peter had bested him. "Then make her eat," was all he said. Then, spinning on his heel, he stalked off in a gloomy mood.

"Peter you need to find…" she broke off in spasms of coughing.

"I know, Charlotte. You have to wait a little longer. Please just…wait." He clasped her hand and brought it to his lips. "I can't live without you."

She made a feeble attempt to snort, "Oh believe me, you could live perfectly fine without my temper. If I pass, remarry and have the new queen take good care of Myla. She needs a mother to raise her."

"And that mother is you!" Peter exclaimed. "Charlotte, please, you have to hold on. Cling to life for your daughter's sake at least!"

She smiled. "I'm trying, Peter. Believe me, I am." Her hand slipped from Peter's and came to rest on his cheek. "Both you and Myla are my reason to cling to life."

He breathed a sigh of relief and kissed her hand. "Thank you."

The patter of footsteps echoed through the hall. Peter recognized the light steps.   Gavin.

He stood up, "Now, your medicine will come soon." He came to the cell door just as Gavin clasped the bars. One hand held a cup of the herb medicine. Peter winced and felt bad that Gavin had risked his life just to bring the wrong herbs. He stuck the cup though the bars. "Here, my king," he said. "Forgive me for taking so long. But my master rarely leaves me alone."

Peter shook his head. "Gavin, I hate to tell you, but, you have been bringing the wrong medicine."

The boy's face faded. "But...but my mother told me this would help. She...she helps many people get well."

"Child, your mother knows nothing of this one herb that is used to cure me," Charlotte's voice called from the back of the cell. "I'm the only one who knows. Your grandmother told me."

Gavin turned back to Peter, waiting for guidance.

"Gavin, you must find a different herb your mother doesn't have. You must find a way to get to Perdita and find lungwort."

"Lungwort?"

"Yes, child. It is the only herb that will cure me fully," Charlotte whispered.

"I could try to get the emperor's apothecary to give me the herb," Gavin suggested. "I could say my master ordered me to get it."

"That would be dangerous, Gavin," Peter said.

"My king, what is more dangerous? Sneaking off or trying to ask the emperor's apothecary for the herbs? Both are life-risking."

The boy had a point. Both would be placing his life on the line. The emperor's apothecary might be the better option to cover up the smuggling. The apothecary wouldn't be as suspicious if Gavin told him his master ordered him to get lungwort. "Very well, I will let you try. Only be careful, Gavin."

"I will try, my king," Gavin replied.

A shout echoed down the hall, making the boy jerk up, eyes wide. "My master." He made a bow and took off running towards the voice.

Peter walked back over to Charlotte and gathered the remaining food. He held it up to her and she frowned at the portion he'd saved.

"Charlotte, you need to eat," he said. "Please, just a little," he coaxed.

She leaned her head against the wall and closed her eyes. She held out a shaking hand. "Fine."

Instead of giving her the bowl he spooned up a little of the white mush and brought it to her mouth. She scowled, obviously unhappy with the fact that she couldn't feed herself.

After some time, she opened her mouth and ate.

———

The night carried no noise. Peter's eyes flew open and he sat up, looking around him. Charlotte lay beside him, head resting on the makeshift pillow he'd made her a while ago.

Nothing seemed out of place, yet something had awakened him. Images of the kidnap ran through his mind. Nothing had seemed wrong then, but their lives had been put in jeopardy and now they were prisoners.

He stood up and, by instinct, groped for the dagger in his boot, the only weapon the enemy hadn't discovered.

A shadowy figure emerged from the darkness bearing a flaming torch. The light made Peter squint and peer at the dark shadow. It was draped in a cloak of black with no hint of who it was. Peter made sure his dagger was behind his back in case the stranger posed a threat. With it's strange dark attire, Peter was sure he didn't have good intentions.

The figure reached into its billowing sleeve. Peter readied himself for a hidden weapon. The shadow must have seen him tense, for it held out it's hand and hissed, "Be still, my king. I bring you no harm."

Peter peered at the figure, "How do I know you are being truthful?"

"I am to be trusted. I am a friend." He revealed a mug from his billowing sleeve. "This will prove to you that I am an ally. In this mug is the needed medicine to heal the queen. Lungwort, just as she said."

Peter approached the shadow with caution and tried to get a look at the figure's face. But it was no good, the shadow was masked in darkness.

The shadow held out the mug and passed it through the cell's bars. "Your young friend can no longer come. I have watched him from a distance and know that his life is in danger. His master will kill him if he thinks the boy is disloyal."

The mention of Gavin being killed made Peter rethink. He assessed the shadow again. "What is my friend's name? If you tell me that, then I will know if you are to be trusted."

"His name is Gavin, son of Rowan and Alice. His master is a powerful general for the emperor of Perdita and will not flinch when he sends the boy to his death."

Peter nodded. He would have to trust the shadow. He had no other means of retrieving the medicine. "Very well, I will trust you," Peter said. "But, if you deceive me, let it be known that if you murder the queen, I will make you pay."

"Understood, my king," the figure said. "Now, I must flee. My life is at risk as well for bringing you the medicine, but the kingdom of Aurum must live. Without it, there will be no light."

The figure swept its garments around and disappeared as quietly as a phantom. Its footfalls never seeming to touch the ground.

Charlotte felt a warm hand rub her shoulder with care. A soothing voice whispered just above her, "Charlotte…"

She opened her eyes to find Peter looking down at her. She heard him breath a sigh of relief and nudged her to a seated position. "I have the medicine you need, love," Peter said.

A rough cylinder was pressed into her hands and she looked down. The darkness hid the image, but the familiar smell filled her nostrils. She closed her eyes and let a wave of hope wash over her. This was the medicine she needed.

She tipped the cup back and let the liquid slide down her sore throat. She couldn't fathom how Peter had gotten the herbs, let alone, make it into the drink. She pushed the questions aside. She would wait for the answers later when they were safe and secure at home.

She put the cup down and looked at Peter. In the dim light, she couldn't see him clearly. After all this time, she longed to see his face again. But his voice and touch were enough to ensure her that he was there and that she was safe. She would see his face soon she hoped. If she could grow stronger they could plan a way to escape.

She reached a hand up and felt for his cheek. The warmth of his skin told her she'd found him. Reaching up with the strength she could muster, she pressed a kiss to his cheek. "Thank you, Peter," she whispered.,"I don't know how you did this, but I'm grateful. I can finally have hope of recovery."

Her throat screamed when she stopped talking. It was the greatest amount of words she'd spoken since she'd gotten ill. She ignored her protesting throat and laid back down.

She heard Peter lay down next to her and wrap an arm around her waist in a protective manner. Before she fell asleep she heard him whisper near her ear, "You know I would do anything to protect you."

———————

From that moment onward Charlotte seemed to gain more strength with each passing hour. The figure continued to bring Peter the medicine and promised to get more whenever Peter traded the empty cup for a full one. The shadow, though mysterious, seemed to bring a light of hope whenever he gave Peter a new cup of herbs.

He watched in amazement as Charlotte's strength returned and she started acting more like her old self. The only thing that was different about her was how affectionate she had become towards him now. She'd never been so forward with her love for him and the difference took him by surprise. Perhaps the sickness had taught her not to rely just on herself for help, but to lean on others in times of darkness. In that respect, Peter was grateful for the change in her.

He sat against the wall one morning and watched Charlotte eat the rest of the portion he'd saved for her. If the guard noticed Charlotte's rising strength he didn't mention it when he brought the meal. He shoved the bowl under the cell door and stalked off with no comment.

Charlotte put the bowl aside half-eaten.

"You're coming along, Charlotte. I must say I'm impressed on how far you've recovered."

She nodded. "I can say the same, Peter," she said, her voice carrying less harshness. "But, you must realize that I still suffer from coughing. You must not let your hopes rise too far, lest they be dashed like a ship in a storm."

Her mouthful of words was enough to convince him her throat wasn't sore. He'd be hearing a lot more from her as the days continued to pass.

With the passing of days came the ever present restlessness of being locked up. He hated the feeling of being trapped and at some tyrannical ruler's mercy. When the phantom came by with the medicine, he'd mentioned trying to help them escape but hadn't brought it up since then.

Heavy footsteps thundered across the hall. Charlotte tensed and looked towards the cell door. Her eyes pierced the bars, waiting for the footfalls to draw closer and for the person to reveal himself.

"Calm yourself, Charlotte," Peter said. "Most likely it's nothing; or perhaps a new cup of medicine." But, inside, Peter knew it wasn't. Those were heavy footsteps. The shadow hardly carried any sound when he approached.

Two figures emerged in the dim light. One small, one large. As they came closer Peter realized it to be the guard.

Right behind him he was dragging a small boy.

Gavin.

Peter shot to his feet. Charlotte remained where she was but watched intently as the guard continued to drag the boy forward. Gavin's clothes were torn and blood was sprayed over his tunic along with grime from work.

The guard stopped at their cell and glared daggers into Peter's gaze. "Clever, o high king," he snarled. "Turning one of our own against us." He unlocked the door and shoved Gavin inside.

Tears streamed down the boy's cheeks. He whimpered when he fell to the ground inside the cell.

"Shut your mouth, boy!" the guard shouted. He slammed the door closed and stalked off.

Peter helped Gavin to a seated position on the floor and knelt beside the crying child, "Gavin, what happened?"

"I'm terribly sorry, my king. But my master found out what I was doing and beat me. Then he decided I should die with the rest of you. A slave who doesn't heed his master's wishes deserves to be put to death." He buried his head in his hand and mumbled, "He said that."

Peter picked the boy up and carried him to Charlotte's side. He watched as she put her arms around Gavin and began to rock him back and forth, humming all the time. "You're safe now, child," she soothed. "The man won't harm you any more."

"But, I don't want to die," Gavin whispered.

"No one wants to, child," Charlotte responded. She picked up the bowl of food she hadn't finished and held it up to him, "Are you hungry? There's some left over."

Gavin nodded, "My master didn't bother to feed me today." He reached out a trembling hand and took the bowl. As he began to eat, Peter went over the scenario.

The shadow had been giving them the medicine, not Gavin. Gavin hadn't come here for a long while. So how had Gavin been found out? Did another servant decide to put the boy in trouble? But what servant would want to bring harm to an innocent boy? Peter knew no answers. Only that now, Gavin was meant to die with them.

Gavin set the empty bowl down and wiped his mouth. He smiled sheepishly at Charlotte, "Thank you, my queen."

"You're welcome, child," she said, pulling him against her. "Now, what exactly is the emperor's plan for us? He can't keep us here for much longer. Why is he waiting so long to kill us?"

Gavin looked as if he might burst into tears again. "He's through with waiting. We die at sunrise the next morning."

Chapter 18

The thundering of several footsteps and clanging of swords echoed through the hall. Peter watched as Gavin jerked from his sleeping position the next morning and gazed worriedly out the cell's bars.

Charlotte straightened and Peter saw her eyes harden as she awaited their enemies. Peter, moved by instincts, pulled himself to his feet and stood in front of Charlotte who had shoved Gavin behind her.

Half a dozen guards all clad with a sword and dagger stopped outside the cell door. The guard who'd watched them since the first day unlocked the door and let the men in. "What exactly do you plan to do with us?" Peter asked, pushing Charlotte back since she'd risen.

"Kill you," one of the guards grunted.

"The emperor will find your deaths both satisfying and entertaining," another one added.

Before Peter could react, the lead guard had his hands bound behind his back and was dragging him out of the cell.

Another guard grabbed Charlotte and started binding her wrists, yanking on the strings to tighten them. A yelp escaped her and Peter yanked against his guard's grip. "Don't you dare harm her!" he spat.

"What can you do?" Charlotte's guard taunted. He grabbed Charlotte's chin and looked down at her. "I still don't see why the emperor would want to close such pretty eyes for eternity."

Charlotte jerked away from him, taking the guard by surprise and bit his finger before he could pull away.

"Arg!" the guard shouted. He grabbed Charlotte again and shoved her out the door, making her stumble to the ground.

Peter moved to help her up but his guard held him fast. "You even dream of harming her, I'll kill you," he hissed. Anger boiled low inside him, waiting to burst forth.

Charlotte managed to pick herself up and glared at her guard through savage green eyes. Her anger was enough to put many people in their place and she used it once again with this guard.

A cry rose from the cell.

Peter turned to see Gavin being dragged out by his bonds and put in line behind Charlotte who stood behind Peter.

"Move on!" the leader ordered.

Peter had no choice but to obey. He started forward, surrounded on all sides by guards. He heard Charlotte cough lightly behind him. Even though she'd gained strength, she still wasn't her normal self. And that worried him the most.

The humming of thousands of people clad in red and black crowded around the outside of the arena. Simon watched as the people began taking their seats on the rocky benches that served as seating.

He'd guessed their death was going to be entertainment for the nobility of Perdita, if there were any noble people in this entire lost city.

A trumpet sounded from above him. He looked up to see a raised balcony overlooking the arena and jutting out to the center of it. Simon guessed that that was where the emperor and his empress sat.

He watched as men in armor filed out onto the balcony. They stood on all sides except the side facing the arena, so as to not block the emperor's view of their tragic deaths.

The emperor strode out, clad in red and black like the other nobles. The only exception was that he wore the colors with such brutality, a shiver ran down Simon's spine. What death awaited them today?

Another trumpet sounded and Simon saw three other people enter the arena. When they drew closer, Simon noticed it to be Peter, Charlotte, and little Gavin.

Alice gasped and Simon saw Rowan hold her back from running towards her child, for guards surrounded the three prisoners.

Charlotte's eyes were on fire and Peter's reflected hers. Simon had never in his life seen the king so upset. He feared Peter would explode at any moment. But, what would the queen do? That was what Simon feared the most. It was no secret the queen had a massive temper. When angered, no one dared cross her path.

The guards led them to where Simon and the rest were positioned in the center. Then they left through the opening from which they had come, which was merely a dark crack in the wall. Once the guards were inside, Alice flung herself at her son and started weeping over him. Rowan knelt beside Gavin as well and hugged his child to his chest, along with his wife.

Simon heard the mocking laughter of the crowd as they watched the scene. He frowned. Why were these people treating them so? Did they realize that they were taking a chance on waging war? If Peter survived, he would most likely want to win Perdita back. After watching the brutal treatment of the town folk, Simon sure hoped Peter did conquer Perdita. But, he was getting ahead of himself. First, Peter had to survive. A matter Simon didn't feel very confident about.

───────────

Peter stared around him at the towering walls of the arena. There was no route of escape. Even if they could scale the walls, guards waited on every corner, daring them to try.

Nobles sat around the arena on stone seats and filled the stadium with mocking laughter. Charlotte stood beside him, her back stiff and her eyes blazing in anger.

He heard her whisper, "This was in my dream. Why didn't I take heed and warn you?"

Even though she seemed to be talking to herself, he wrapped an arm around her middle and pulled her closer. She seemed to relax, but only a little. She still remained erect and firm. He leaned toward her ear. "Everything will be fine, Charlotte."

She gave him a dubious look but didn't fire back a retort.

A fanfare filled the air and Peter looked up to where the emperor sat and saw a lady clad in a fine, blue silken dress sweep onto the balcony. She caught Peter's eye and smirked.

A sense of foreboding fell over him as he stared up at the woman. She had the air of a supreme leader used to getting her way. Her blue eyes penetrated his very soul and filled it with dread. But who was she? And what did she have in mind for them?

Charlotte must have also sensed the dread-filled atmosphere for she tensed up again. She stared at the woman with her intense green eyes and refused to waiver. The lady, whoever she was, seemed to disturb Charlotte, making Peter rise on his defensive side as well.

The emperor stood and offered the woman a kiss on her hand and guided her to a seat next to him. He strode to the edge of the balcony and raised his hands. "My fellow noblemen and lovely ladies!" he announced. "It is my greatest pleasure to put on this execution for you. My lovely empress and I will finally see our enemy fall and I am honored to be the one to conduct such an event."

Cheers rose up from the crowd. Peter stood in confusion. How were they the emperor's enemy?

He could bare it no longer. He stepped forward, offering Charlotte encouragement through a quick squeeze of her hand. "How are we your enemy?" he demanded.

The emperor put his hands on the balcony and leaned down. "Ah, so our prisoner finally wants to know who hunted him all these years. Well, I say we give him his answers before death, shall we?"

The crowd responded with more cheers.

The empress stood up and joined her husband by the balcony's edge. "King Peter, we are pleased to finally meet you, King Philip's squire. I thought you would know about us, but perhaps not."

She offered him a sweet smile, dripping with poison. "We have been loathing the kingdom ever since we broke away. King Philip destroyed our dream for independence. So we made our own empire outside his kingdom and plotted to take Aurum by force when we were ready." The empress hung her head as if in mock guilt. "But, sadly, our plans failed when she tried to steal the kingdom. Morgana was like a sister to me."

Peter stared at the empress in shock. Was that how Morgana had gathered her mass army? Was she in league with the emperor of Perdita? It suddenly made sense.

"But, alas she died!" the empress exclaimed, flinging her arms up. She shot Charlotte a deadly glare. "Murdered by her own wretched daughter!"

Charlotte seared the empress with her gaze but the wince she gave didn't escape Peter. Her eyes never wavered from the empress but they were misted over like she was about to cry.

He pulled her to him again this time hugging her, "You mistake who you speak of. Charlotte is the most beautiful woman I have ever laid eyes on. Her heart is as pure as her appearance. You and the emperor, are not so."

He saw the empress' eyes flare and thought he heard her huff. She spun on her heel and returned to her seat.

The emperor continued to stare down at him.

"Another question. Who brought us here?" Peter demanded. "Who let you know we were here?"

The emperor snorted, "King Peter, it is the one who watched you since the kidnapping that led you to this forsaken land."

"Who?" Peter asked, his patience wearing thin.

The emperor jerked his head to one of the guards.

Peter watched as the last person he expected came forward from behind the guard.

Captain Sadon.

"You?" Peter asked.

Captain Sadon shrugged, "I remain loyal to the emperor. He offered a high reward to bring you here. I agreed."

Peter was astounded at the fact that he'd let himself trust this man. Sadon had known they were there and where they needed to go to find Myla. Why didn't he suspect him?

Charlotte gasped aloud, "How could you?" She walked forward. "You led us to believe you were helping us. In the end, you deceived us."

Her words seemed not to shake the captain. He only shrugged. "I did what I had to do."

"Does money truly mean more to you than loyalty and truthfulness? Do you not see the pain your people live through? If you love money so much give it to your town."

The emperor and Sadon exchanged glances. "I see you have a strong resentment of money," the emperor replied.

Sadon only stared.

"I don't resent money," Charlotte replied. "Only the people who misuse it and bring pain to others from it. You don't deserve it if you only want to use it against your own people."

The emperor scowled. "You have strong opinions for a woman. I see you only as a threat. You, the king, and the rest of your servants will die. I have no more use for you."

"Wait!" Charlotte shouted. "Before you kill me, one more question!"

The emperor turned. "Yes?"

"Where is my daughter?"

The emperor let out a mocking laugh. He jerked his head to a wet nurse and Peter saw that she carried a bundle in her arms.

He watched as the emperor plucked the babe from the nurse's arms and by both his hands dangled her above their heads.

Charlotte screeched and Peter caught her before she acted in her anger.

He ran so he stood below Myla in case the emperor decided to drop her. Charlotte followed. "Don't mistreat my daughter like that!" he shouted.

Myla began to scream and kick. The emperor jerked her back up and handed her to the nurse. "Don't worry about your child, King Peter. I will make sure she grows up to become a ruthless ruler fit to wear a crown. And," he added, plucking another child from a different nurse, "this little one, her brother calls, Faye, will be the princess' maidservant."

Alice shrieked and Rowan hugged her to him in order to stop her from hurting herself. "Oh, my baby!" Alice cried.

Peter gave Rowan a sympathetic look as his steward comforted his wife.

The emperor handed the children back to the nurses and took his seat. "Now, you die."

Raising his hands he shouted, "Release Occisor!"

A grated metal gate began to rise. As the gap grew larger and larger, Peter began to see smoke seep through the crack.

The crowd oohed and began to clap.

The smoke spread around them. Peter pushed Charlotte behind him and backed away from the dark cloud.

Rowan did the same with Alice who clutched Gavin near her skirts. Simon looked around him cautiously and kept peering into the smoke. His eyes widened.

Peter turned back to the gap in the wall and saw a flicker of movement within. He froze. Charlotte peered around his shoulder but he moved in front of her.

Flames erupted from nowhere and sprayed across the arena.

Peter flung himself on the ground, taking Charlotte with him. The hot fire shot where his face used to be. He dared a glance up.

Long, black claws appeared from the smoke. Blood red scales appeared next. Peter rose keeping his eyes on the strange legs.

A face he knew he'd see in his nightmares emerged and stared at Peter with golden eyes.

Charlotte caught her breath behind him. "A dragon," she whispered.

Not one of them moved. They were frozen in place, afraid of what the beast would do if they even breathed.

Peter continued to stare at the beast. The dragon did the same to him. The reptile sent off a flicking tongue and studied Peter, then Charlotte, and finally Rowan, Alice, Gavin, and Simon behind them.

The crowd erupted into roars at the sight of the beast.

The dragon seemed to finish the study of his meal for he began to move around them. Peter watched as the beast's tail curled around his whole group.

Gavin whimpered and Alice clutched her son closer. Rowan watched the tail with Simon as they waited for the beast to attack.

The beast encircled them and, content with the meal in his clutches he raised his head to the sky and let out an ear piercing roar.

The crowd answered with more cheers.

The dragon shot fire into the sky, sending it falling towards them.

"Run!" Peter shouted. "Take cover!"

No one had to be told twice. They raced for the dragon's cavern only to have the gate shut on them. They were now trapped in the arena with a hungry beast who most likely wanted to make his meal suffer before killing it.

Gavin started to cry and Alice picked him up.

Simon joined Peter and Charlotte, keeping an eye on the dragon still shooting fire into the sky. "Peter, what do we do?"

"Do you want to die?" Peter asked.

"Of course not!"

"Do you have a weapon of any sort?"

Simon dug a dagger from his boot. "Will this do?"

Peter shrugged. "It's better than nothing." He retrieved his own. "The only way we're going to survive is if we kill that beast."

"How?" Simon asked. "Have you seen that creature?"

"Of course I have! And I don't know. We have to try, at least."

A wooden sheet fell from above them. Ruins from the dragon's fire? Peter didn't care. He ran to where the piece of wood was while the dragon was distracted. Simon and Rowan moved to help him.

They dragged it to the side where Charlotte, Alice, and Gavin crouched.

Propping the sheet against the arena's wall, Peter gestured for them to hide behind it. "Take cover here. As long as the beast doesn't see you he won't come after you. Rowan, stay here and make sure the beast doesn't hurt them."

"Where are you going?" Charlotte asked.

"Putting an end to this slaughter," Peter said, showing her his dagger. "I have to try at least. If I die..." he didn't finish.

Charlotte gripped his shoulders. "You will not die," she said.

He brought her hand to his lips. "Stay safe, Charlotte. Don't come out."

With that, he turned away towards the beast with Simon by his side. He nodded that he was ready.

Peter glanced down at the dagger in his hand. What he truly needed was a sword. This knife wouldn't kill the beast in one jab, which made the job much harder.

"I'll need you to watch my back. If this beast attacks, I'll not come out in one piece."

Simon gulped and nodded.

The beast finally stopped his fire show and turned his attention to the two men approaching it. The beast growled at Peter and began to crawl towards him.

Peter's mind whispered to him as death made its way towards him. *You are Lord Protector over your kingdom.*

The dragon hissed and spit sparks in his direction.

Peter's mind continued. *Your wife and daughter's lives are in your hands. Aurum's future is at stake.* He gripped the dagger and waited for the dragon to edge closer.

"Go on, Occisor!" the empress yelled. "Finish him!"

The beast lit up in fury and Peter dodged aside as fire sprayed where he used to stand. He ran to the other side of the arena, Simon on his heels.

The dragon turned towards him and crawled over, its tail wrapped around, encircling them in a prison of red. The beast lashed out like a serpent, making Peter jump back and slash the monster on the muzzle.

The dragon roared and stumbled back, but was on them again in an instant. The beast whipped its tail, catching Peter off guard. He jumped to avoid being tripped but watched Simon fall with a grunt.

The knight stumbled to a standing position. His eyes widened. "Peter, look out!"

Peter felt searing pain jolt through his legs as he felt himself falling towards the hard earth.

———————

"Peter!" Charlotte shouted. Her husband fell with a loud thud and the beast stood over him hissing.

It let out an enraged yowl. Simon had slashed its back and was going for another attack. The beast growled and used its tail as a whip, sending Simon across the arena and slamming him into the wall. The knight fell and didn't get up.

Gavin cowered near Rowan, hiding his face in his father's chest. Alice gasped and did the same as her child.

Charlotte's anger at this revolting game surged to life. She never dreamed it would come to this. Drawing her dagger, she stood. She could feel her strength draining. Before she was completely helpless, she needed to do something.

"My queen, you can't go out there!" Rowan exclaimed. "Give me your dagger and I'll help your husband."

She shot Rowan a glare. "No, stay here with Alice and your child. I have a different way to go about this." She pressed the dagger into Rowan's hand. "You need this more than I do."

"Whatever do you mean?" Rowan asked. "You're going after the beast. You should have this."

"No, I have something else in mind."

Rowan pressed the dagger back into Charlotte's hand. "Your Majesty, I insist." Charlotte only nodded and looked towards the dragon. It was again standing over Peter, ready to offer the killing bite.

Sheathing the weapon, she started to run towards the beast. With all her experience with mythical creatures, a dragon couldn't be any different. Just like she did with the phoenix and the griffins, she'd train and use this beast against her enemies.

The griffins. If only Luna and Ferox were here. She'd seen no sign of them since the ambush.

"Stop!" she yelled at the massive beast.

It snapped its attention to her and hissed. It studied her with fiery eyes.

"Occisor, step aside!" she ordered.

To her surprise the beast obeyed. It stepped away from Peter and came towards her.

"Charlotte, get away from that beast!" Peter shouted at her. He was beginning to stand, holding his shoulder.

She ignored him and watched the dragon, challenging it to disobey. She held out her hand and started toward it.

It hissed but didn't attack.

If she could just touch it. Show her she wasn't a threat. Merely show it who was in control. Then, it would listen to every command she voiced.

Her legs were weakening but she had to remain strong.

Her hand was almost touching the dragon's muzzle.

A scream of outrage came from above, and Charlotte recognized the empress' voice.

The dragon narrowed its eyes and drew away from Charlotte. It let out a roar and Charlotte watched in horror as fire came straight at her.

———————

"No!" Peter shouted as he watched Charlotte collapse on the ground at the dragon's feet. The flames had scorched the ground around Charlotte and, from this distance, he couldn't tell if Charlotte was burned. But, he felt the sizzling heat.

The emperor and empress' moving laughter filled the air. Peter could feel hot blood rise in his veins; this time it wasn't just from the fire.

He charged towards the beast, his dagger in his hand. The dragon seemed startled by his yell and backed away from Charlotte's crumpled form. Peter dropped to the ground beside her.

Her beautiful eyes were closed and her dress was scorched. Without thinking, he pulled her up against his chest and buried his face in her hair. "Lord, please no. Not again," he whispered. "Don't take her away from me."

She stirred and he took his head away. Her eyelids fluttered open and she looked up at him. "Peter," she whispered.

He hugged her. "Oh, thank the Lord."

She stiffened and Peter noticed the dragon was over its shock and was hissing while moving towards them. Peter saw Charlotte position her dagger, ready to fling it towards the beast. He nodded and moved his body aside slightly.

The dragon flung itself at them.

Charlotte tossed the dagger straight and true. The knife sunk into the dragon's scales and it screeched its protest to the sky. It backed away from them and started trying to pry the weapon from its chest.

"Missed," Charlotte whispered.

Peter looked closer. The dagger was meant to stab the dragon's heart. It was off by a mere nudge. He looked at her then his dagger. He squeezed her hand. "I'll be right back."

She returned the squeeze and offered him a smile.

He stood and made his way towards the wounded beast.

The dragon caught sight of him and stopped trying to take the knife out of its scales. It hissed in anger and charged at him. Sparks spit out of its mouth, making Peter dodge them the best he could.

A flame caught on his doublet and he beat it out, clenching his teeth. He ducked when the tail came swinging at him from the sky. Readying his dagger, he eyed the dragon's chest.

The dragon was almost on top of him.

He ducked when another whip from the tail came his way.

The beast knocked him on his back and stood over him like before.

"Peter!" he heard Charlotte screech.

"Go on, Occisor!" encouraged the emperor.

Peter arranged his dagger and, when the dragon made a snap for his neck, he drove it into the beast's black heart.

The blood dripping on his face told him the beast was dying.

It was roaring and swinging its neck from side to side. Then, it began to fall.

Peter rolled out from under the dragon just before the beast's body hit the ground. He wiped the blood from his face and looked at the dead creature.

Charlotte flung herself at him and he hugged her close. Only when she was shaking did he realize she was weeping. He looked to see Rowan, Alice, and Gavin come out from the wooden shelter. His gaze went to Simon still unmoving on the ground. He winced. He needed to make sure his knight was still alive.

"No!" the emperor roared.

The empress was screaming and pointing at some of the guards. Peter couldn't decipher what she said but it didn't sound promising.

Suddenly, the dragon's cell was opened and a mass of soldiers spilled out. They were charging straight at them.

"You haven't cheated death!" the emperor roared. "I will have my way and you and your whole company will die!"

Peter glanced at his bloody dagger.

Charlotte clung to his hand and he realized her dagger was still beneath the beast.

The army charged forward.

Peter readied himself to face his enemy head-on, when a familiar screech split the air.

Chapter 19

Charlotte looked above the mass of soldiers' heads at the tunnel they'd come from. The screeching kept on coming from the opening. The men started to turn around in confusion at the sound.

Charlotte smiled. She knew that sound. But, was it truly real?

Peter gripped her hand and pointed at the tunnel. "Look, Charlotte."

Bursting from the opening, two pitch black creatures ran out screeching at the army.

Chaos broke out among the men. They began scrambling away from the attacking beasts that charged at them. Luna knocked two men to the ground and came to Charlotte's side. She wrapped her tail around her and Peter.

Ferox was by Alice and Rowan's side, hissing at anyone who dared to go near.

The emperor was screaming at his men to attack, but it seemed to fall on deaf ears. The men wouldn't approach the griffins.

Charlotte took the advantage and pointed to the reluctant men. "Luna, attack," she ordered.

At the familiar command, the black griffin leapt into battle. Men screamed in pain as they were attacked. Ferox did her part by protecting the others and snapped at anyone who stumbled near her.

Peter grabbed Charlotte's hand and squeezed it. "I'll be right back."

She kept hold of his hand. "Where are you going?"

He motioned to Simon lying on the ground. "I need to see if he's still breathing."

As soon as she nodded, he took off running to the knight's side.

Peter knelt beside Simon and felt the knight's pulse. It beat slowly. Peter breathed a sigh of relief. He was still alive.

Seeing the men were still occupied with Luna, he dragged Simon to Alice and Rowan's side. Gavin's little eyes widened. "What happened?" he asked, his lip trembling.

Peter rubbed the boy's shoulder. "He's fine, Gavin. He's only unconscious." He met Rowan's eyes. "I just need him here for protection."

Rowan nodded, "Of course. What can I do to help?"

Peter shook his head. "We're helpless without weapons." He glanced down at the dagger in his hand. "This won't do much."

A screech of terror filled his ears. Peter squinted at the piercing noise and looked into the mass of chaos.

He saw Luna, blood flowing down her leg and spilling onto the ground. The griffin, outraged, grabbed the man in her beak and flung him across the arena. The man crashed into the wall beside Peter and fell, unconscious.

Peter jumped to the man's side and tugged the man's sword from his limp grasp. He handed his dagger to Rowan. "Keep this. I'll get you a sword shortly."

He ran into the fray and stabbed the first man he reached. The man howled and fell to the ground. Peter grabbed his adversary's sword and tossed it to Rowan.

Peter saw his steward press the dagger into Alice's trembling hands, kiss her, hug Gavin, and charged into battle. He came up alongside Peter and started hacking down the men with Peter.

The emperor was screaming and Peter picked up the words, "Take cover!" and "princess". He looked up to find the empress grabbing Myla and running towards the opening. The nurse did the same with Faye. His eyes widened. If the empress managed to get inside, they'd lose the girls.

He glanced at Ferox still by Alice and Gavin. "Ferox!" he shouted.

Recognizing her name, the griffin cocked her head at Peter. "Myla, Ferox! Go get Myla!"

As an answer, the griffin took off and whipped over to the emperor's balcony. The guards near the emperor shrieked as Ferox started attacking them. The griffin charged straight at the empress.

Peter heard the cries of terror from the women.

Ferox emerged from the booth, carrying both Myla and Faye in her grasp. She soared over to Alice and dropped Faye in the crying mother's arms. Peter watched Alice hug Ferox and nuzzle Myla, who still hung from the griffin's jaws screaming.

Ferox trotted over to Peter, careful not to trip on the dead bodies. She presented him with his princess with pride. Peter plucked the crying babe from the griffin and cuddled her in his arms. He stroked Ferox's ears, tears coming to his eyes. "Thank you, Ferox," he said.

Then, hugging Myla to him, he sprinted back to where Charlotte stood with Luna. Charlotte had an enemy's sword in hand and was doing her best to ward off any foes. But, Peter noticed her slouching shoulders. Soon, she would pass out. Her body, still battling sickness, was not equipped to fight.

"Charlotte," he said, coming to her side.

Her eyes widened at the sight of Myla in his arms. She let her sword clatter to the ground. "Myla!" she exclaimed. She threw her arms around Peter and took Myla from him. She brought her face to Myla's and nuzzled her. "Oh, my child, you're safe," she whispered. Myla had stopped crying and was only whimpering as Charlotte held her. Charlotte looked up at Peter, her eyes wet, "How did you manage to get to her?"

"I will tell you later," he said, "I promise." He whistled and Luna came to his side. "Get on Luna's back with Alice, Gavin, and Faye. Get as far from here as you can. I'll come to you when I finish this."

She looked at him with wide eyes.

"But, you must promise me something," he said.

"What?" her voice barley audible.

"If I don't return before the sun sets, you leave without me."

She stood back. "No!" she shouted. "No, I won't go anywhere. I will stay by your side until this is over. I…"

"You have to think of Myla, Charlotte. It's not just you, it's her as well. Along with Alice and Faye. You have to escape while you have a chance."

Charlotte looked over to where Ferox joined Rowan to ward off the men near Alice. Gavin clutched Alice's dress and hid his face in the folds. She brought her eyes up to meet his gaze. "Very well. But I will wait for you."

"If I'm back by sunset. If not...you leave. Clear?" He could tell she was trying hard not to cry. Her eyes were an ocean of unshed tears.

"We're clear," she said, her voice broke, betraying her stoic appearance.

He swept her up in one last embrace. He nuzzled into her hair and let his mind capture this moment. It could very well be his last with her. Cupping her cheek, he pressed his mouth to hers and savored one last kiss before he went into battle.

Pulling away, he kissed Myla on the forehead. "Now go," he ordered.

Charlotte hugged Myla close and swung up on Luna's back. He watched as Luna flew to Alice's side and let the woman scramble up her back. Charlotte sat in the front with Myla while Gavin sat in front of Alice and Faye lay in her mother's arms. Charlotte signaled Ferox to remain and gave Luna another sign.

Luna raised her massive wings and took to the sky.

———————

Charlotte watched as Peter's figure got smaller and smaller as she ascended. She forced the oncoming tears back and focused on leading Luna away from the arena. Alice gripped Charlotte's waist from behind. She could hear her friend's shaken breathing and stifled sobs. Charlotte knew Alice was trying her best to hide her worry and grief for her husband as well.

"Don't worry so, Alice. Rowan will be back. Peter will make sure everyone gets out of that arena. Even if he pays with his own life." Tears sprang up again when she stated the last remark. She didn't want Peter to have to do that, but she knew he would. She knew he would never leave his fellow soldiers to die in the hands of an enemy. He would sacrifice himself just to let everyone else escape.

She shoved her tears back again and tried not to dwell on such thoughts. She needed to stay focused.

Yelling met her ears from down below.

Alice gasped and clung harder onto Faye and Gavin.

Charlotte's breath caught in her throat.

The emperor's soldiers were aiming large ballistas straight at them.

Charlotte gripped Myla tighter and steered Luna in circles, hoping to confuse the men.

The tactic worked for a few moments, but the soldiers grew smarter and pointed many ballistas in different directions; each one waiting to fire.

Charlotte knew they'd shoot them down. Their intent was to kill them. How they were going to retrieve Myla alive, she had no idea. But, the emperor had his ways.

She heard the click of the large weapons below.

She squeezed Luna's scruff and twisted it slightly. "Hold on tight, Alice," she ordered. "When I tell Luna to rise, she doesn't hesitate."

Alice responded by holding her children close and tightening her grip on Charlotte's waist.

More weapon's clicked and lay poised to fire.

Now.

With a jerk, she commanded, "Rise, Luna."

The griffin didn't hesitate. With a flurry of motion, the griffin's wings lifted them higher into the sky.

The whistle of the ballistas' arrows echoed around them.

Luna continued to climb higher.

Once out of range, Charlotte turned the griffin towards the sea.

Soon, the arena was out of sight.

———————

Echoed screams pierced his blank mind. Simon lifted his head and peered around. Chaos filled the atmosphere. Men screamed and fell in pain, blood flowing from wounds. A massive black beast attacked anything near it.

His mind was a blur. Where was he? What had happened to him?

He caught sight of a familiar figure fighting with a soldier clad in black and red. The young man's brown hair and yelling voice echoed in his mind.

Then, he remembered…everything.

That was Peter. They were still in the arena, where he'd warned Peter of the...his eyes fell on the corpse of the dragon. Yes, he was still here. Rowan was behind Peter, defending the king's back. Ferox, Simon recognized was taking the most men down with her quick attacks and massive size. But, Simon noticed blood running down both the griffin's front legs. Soon, she'd lose her ability to fight.

Simon took advantage of the mens' ignorance of him and sat up. A wave of dizziness crashed over him and he had to close his eyes. After the motion subsided, he tried to stand. A dizzy wave flowed through his mind once again. He shut his eyes once more until it passed.

Then, charging into the battle, he attacked the first man he made contact with.

———————

Charlotte landed near the port in the deserted town. Perdita remained as it did the first day they arrived. Nothing had changed.

Alice slid to the ground and began to comfort her children who were trembling.

Charlotte copied her example and bounced Myla up and down. But, Myla seemed content just to stay on Luna. Myla ran her tiny fingers through the griffin's black, glossy fur and cooed in delight.

Charlotte smiled at her daughter's delight. At least her baby didn't realize what a life and death predicament they were in. She didn't want Myla to be worried like she was. Charlotte glanced at the sky.

The sun was starting to sink, painting the sky beautiful colors of pink, orange, and purple. Peter had told her to start back if he wasn't back by sunset. Tears sprang up into her eyes. She didn't want to leave him. She couldn't. Charlotte looked around. Nothing stirred. There was no sign of the enemy. She made up her mind. She'd wait a little longer. It wouldn't hurt anyone if the enemy wasn't in sight.

"Charlotte, what's that?" Alice's voice trembled as well as her finger that was pointing to a dark street.

Shadows flitted back and forth in the alley. Charlotte leaned forward and peered into the darkness. Her grip on Myla tightened at the sight that met her eyes.

At least two dozen soldiers filtered out of the alley; each carrying a crossbow.

Charlotte's insides groaned.

One soldier raised his crossbow and pointed it at her head.

Chapter 20

With a final scream, the arena went silent. Peter looked up from the man he'd just slain. The arena's seats were vacant, as was the balcony. The emperor must have retreated while they were still fighting. He looked at Rowan and Simon. Rowan had a sliced tunic and his arms were cut. However, most of his steward's wounds didn't seem to be serious. Simon had blood matted in his hair from his fall and blood seeped through his tunic around his shoulders and arms.

Simon's eyes widened at Peter, making Peter look down at his own doublet and tunic. Red covered more of the leather and fabric than the clothing's colors. Since the fighting had began, he finally felt fire burn up his arms from the strenuous battle. Pain flowed up his arms and he guessed he had a few cuts and bruises. "Don't worry, Simon," he reassured, "this blood isn't all mine."

Simon seemed to take the statement as true because the knight blew out a sigh.

Rowan nodded to the stands. "If we wish to leave, I suggest we leave now. Plus, the sun is making its final goodbye."

Peter looked up at the sky. Fiery red and orange lit the atmosphere. Charlotte would be worried about him. He whistled for Ferox. Ferox trotted from the pile of dead bodies she stood over and came to his side. She let out a guttural noise and spread her wings. Peter hoisted himself onto her back and gave Rowan and Simon a hand up. "Let's start for home," he announced.

"Give us that child," one of the soldiers ordered.

Charlotte clung to Myla tightly. "Why would I do that?" she asked, narrowing her eyes. "There is not a force in this world that would make me hand my child over to that tyrant you call your emperor."

The soldier only chuckled at her anger. "Then we'll kill you. It's that simple. We'll take her either way." He cocked his brows. "So, o great queen," he taunted, "what will it be? Do you want to live and give us the baby or die and we still keep the babe?"

Alice was starting to whimper softly.

Charlotte glared at the soldiers. "If I give you my child, you are to leave my friend's children alone."

"Fine by me. The emperor only wants the princess."

A screech pierced the sky.

Charlotte looked up to see Peter riding Ferox. Tears filled her eyes. This time they weren't from grief. Ferox landed beside Luna and Peter jumped down, drawing his sword. "What is the meaning of this?" he asked in a growl. "I killed your fellow soldiers and I'll do the same here."

Charlotte slid to the ground and came to Peter's side.

"I don't care how many men you slaughtered," the soldier retorted. Ripples of agreement echoed through the other soldiers. "Give us the princess."

More echoed their agreements.

"Or," the soldier said, pointing his crossbow at Peter. "Die."

Charlotte grabbed Peter's hand and squeezed, willing him to tread with caution.

Peter bent to her ear. His breath kissed her ear as he whispered, "All will be well."

"How?" she asked.

As he opened his mouth to respond a flurry of motion surrounded them.

Figures clad in black cloaks encircled the emperor's soldiers and drew their swords. Charlotte looked around her. They were surrounded by this strange, silent force. Her first thought was a band of outlaws. But, then why did they seem to take their side? Unless, of course, they wanted Peter and the rest of them to themselves.

"What's this?" the lead soldier demanded.

One figure stepped out from the mass of dark shapes. It approached on silent feet and, as an answer, attacked the soldier with a hidden sword.

It took Peter a few moments to fully understand their new situation. The shadows were swiping out hidden swords and attacking the soldiers with swift blows. The leader of the shadowy figures still attacked the general of the army and forced him back.

Peter knew then that he recognized the shadow leader as the one who'd brought the medicine to Charlotte. He wore the same cloak he'd had when he delivered the lungwort. Meaning, he and his band of men were on their side. Peter drew the sword he'd taken from the emperor and ran to help force the enemy back. Rowan and Simon joined him.

As he cut down the third man, Peter noticed the leader run his sword through the general's stomach. The general's features twisted in pain as he collapsed, dead. Seeing their general dead and realizing they were outnumbered, the remaining soldiers backed away.

"Retreat!" one soldier screeched. "There's too many of them!"

The others didn't need to be told again. They spun on their heels and charged back into the alleyway where they'd come from.

Simon let out a victorious whoop and shook his fist in the air. "We've done it again!" he shouted. "And for the final time!"

Rowan joined Alice again and gathered his family in a hug, laughing.

Peter smiled and turned to see Charlotte running towards him with Myla. He caught her in his arms and let himself revel in this moment. Victory was theirs at last.

He felt Charlotte trembling and pulled away. "Are you crying?" he asked.

She shook her head and let out a bubble of laughter. "No, I'm laughing."

"But there's tears in yours eyes."

"They're tears of joy, not sorrow."

He smiled down at her. Myla let out a squeal and lifted her arms towards him. He laughed and scooped her up. Swinging her around, he listened to her gurgling laughter for the first time in a while.

Another laughing met his ears.

He spun around and only then noticed the shadowy figures were still there. The leader was the one laughing.

Peter approached the figure. "Thank you for what you've done."

The shadow nodded, "It is our pleasure, my king. We are your faithful servants till the end."

Peter frowned, "If you are to be, then I wish to know who you are."

The figure chuckled again. "Very well, you have a right to know."

The shadow pulled back his hood and Peter gaped at the familiar face.

Giles.

Peter watched as the other shadows pushed aside their hoods revealing the sailors from the *Ventus Amicus*. He must have been caught gaping along with the others, for Giles laughed.

"I see we have surprised our great king, men," he said.

"You have done just that," Peter said. "It was you all along. But, what about the captain?"

Giles shook his head. "Sadon chose money over friendship. Greed blinded him from seeing the true nobility. All he thought about was the money."

"Did you know this when we set sail with you?" Peter asked.

Giles shook his head again. "I knew nothing until we docked. I overheard Sadon speaking with the emperor's men. He said he planned to ambush you. When I heard this, I knew I had to act. I couldn't stand by and let you be killed."

"I appreciate your concern, Giles," Peter replied. "Your quick acting saved all of our lives and reunited our families."

Giles bowed, "It is an honor." He nodded to a ship twice the size of the *Ventus Amicus*. "Shall we take you home?"

Chapter 21

The rise and fall of the ship, *Fidelium,* no longer bothered Peter as he watched Charlotte rock Myla back and forth. Cooing to her child, she paced the room, trying to get Myla to fall asleep.

Peter leaned against the doorframe and smiled at her loving nature with their daughter. He'd known she loved Myla from the day their child had entered the world. But, Charlotte was always one to keep her love private. She never expressed her true feelings to anyone in public. It was rare even for Peter to have seen her express her love for Myla when he entered the room. She would smile and hand her to Peter when he asked but seemed distant when she did.

Now, everything was different. He continued to watch her sing softly to their baby and rock her gently whenever Myla started to whimper.

A breeze filled their cabin and Peter closed his eyes briefly and savored the cool evening. Giles had given them the best cabin on board, saying it was his way of making up for their treatment in the emperor's dungeon. The cabin was on the top deck with a small, private balcony overlooking the sea. Two, wide doors opened up to the balcony and currently lay open, letting the breeze into the snug room.

Charlotte laid Myla down in her little cradle, speaking softly when Myla whimpered. "Go to sleep, my child. It's time for you to rest." Charlotte looked up from Myla's cradle and offered him a sweet smile.

When she glided over to him, he pushed himself off the doorframe and gathered her hands in his. "And how is my beautiful queen this evening?"

Charlotte smiled and looked down at her feet. "I'm well, thank you, Peter. My health is close to being fully restored. I only suffer from weakness when I overwork."

Peter frowned and brought her hand to his lips. "You mustn't work too much. You need rest more than anything else."

"I will be fine, Peter," Charlotte reassured him. "I know how to care for myself."

He led her to the balcony and looked out at the setting sun on the horizon. The fiery sky reflected upon the ocean and set the water afire. The beauty was breathtaking. He pulled her closer and continued to gaze out at the vast expanse of water. Oh what he would give to be back home, in his own stronghold. Despite the beauty around him, he wanted to be at home in Aurum.

Charlotte surprised him by resting her head on his shoulder and snuggling closer to him. He didn't need to second guess that this trip had changed Charlotte's view of love and dependency on others. And he could tell her love for him and Myla had deepened. She expressed her love to him more often. Instead of pulling away from him, she drew closer.

Peter's thoughts drifted back to the people of Perdita. They still suffered in their emperor's tyrannical hands. Now that he'd learned the land used to belong to King Philip, perhaps he'd discuss waging war to earn the land back. When he got back home he'd bring up the matter with the Council. He couldn't bear to leave those people with that greedy emperor. That type of man didn't deserve to have so much power. He only hoped Charlotte would give her consent and allow him to go alone. He wouldn't drag her into another war. He couldn't bear to have her suffer more brutality. She'd seen enough of that as a child and young adult.

———————

Charlotte stared across the water at the dying sun. She felt the heat of Peter's body next to her and his arms around her waist. She rested her cheek against him and looked back on recent days. Her health had improved and she was prepared to face whatever trials came their way head-on. As she recalled the memories of her sickness, she realized that she wouldn't have made it through without Peter or Alice. They'd made sure that she ate or took her medicine. Peter had made her as comfortable as possible in their cell and made sure she was warm at night.

She'd come to regret her harsh treatment of them in the previous years. It's not that she didn't trust them. She did, with her life. But, she never opened up fully to them. She'd been afraid to get hurt and lose them. She'd lost so many people in her life she couldn't bear any more heartbreak.

But, the sickness had opened her eyes. It had shown her it wasn't right to push people away who wanted to help her. She should learn to trust people and allow them to contribute to whatever seemed to be troubling her.

She felt Peter shift his weight and she looked up at him. His eyes stared out at the horizon. His gaze was troubled.

She frowned. "What is it, Peter?" she asked. "You look worried."

His gaze shifted to hers, "I'm only thinking."

"About what?"

He looked back at the water, "About Perdita and how much the people there need a new ruler."

She realized where this was going. "You want to declare war?"

He looked down at his boots. "Yes, I believe so. King Philip used to rule the area and I believe we should have it back. It rightfully belongs to Aurum."

Her heart filled with sadness at the thought of him leaving again. She wanted him to stay home. She wanted him with her and Myla. She wanted him to watch Myla grow up. She shook the thoughts away. She was being selfish. She knew the people of Perdita needed a savior. They didn't deserve to be ruled by such a greedy man.

Peter turned away from the sunset and faced her. Kneeling down in front of her he took her hand, "I will not go without your agreement. You will not be allowed to come with me, but I will not go unless you give your consent."

She touched his head and ran her fingers through his hair. "I give you my consent."

He got up. "Truly?"

"Yes, truly." Charlotte brought her hand to touch his cheek. "Those people need to be rescued. I can think of no better person than yourself to save them."

He smiled, "Then I will brooch the subject to the Council as soon as we return."

She held up her hand. "On one condition."

"Oh? And what may I ask is that?"

"That you return to me and Myla victorious or not. I want you to be able to see Myla grow." Charlotte leaned against him. "And I want you by my side for the rest of my life."

He pulled her away and she looked up to see him smiling. "I'm glad you want me to come back. I want both the things you mentioned." His mouth tightened. "But, I can't give you a false promise. War is a dangerous and disastrous matter. It leaves destruction and heartache wherever it goes."

"Then you must promise to try," Charlotte said.

He brought her hands to his lips and kissed both of them. "That I can do."

Epilogue

12 years later

A whistle pierced the air. An arrow shot straight and true through the air and sank into the blood colored center of the target.

A squeal of delight filled the inner bailey.

Peter looked up from where he leaned against a large tree to see Myla jumping up and down. She was pointing to the target. "Look, Father!" she shouted. "Do you see that? I shot that arrow!"

"Yes, I do see," Peter said, rising. "Well done, Daughter. Your archery skill still amazes me. Your mother taught you well."

Myla spun in a circle, doing a victory dance. "When I grow up I shall be the best archer in all of Aurum!" She laughed and fixed another arrow into her longbow. Taking up her position once more, she shot another arrow at the target. The arrow sank into the center again. Peter smiled with pride. His daughter rarely missed her target.

Charlotte had insisted on teaching Myla how to shoot and their daughter had quickly risen to the top, even beating many of the squires. Myla possessed a natural talent with archery and Peter knew that would serve her well in the years to come.

"Fadda!" a young boy's voice filled the air.

Peter turned from where he watched Myla and saw his three year old son tottering towards him, Charlotte walking behind him making sure the child didn't trip.

Peter smiled and knelt down opening his arms. His son fell into them and Peter hoisted him up. He ruffled the boy's brown hair and held him close.

Charlotte came to stand by him. "Arthur, you must be carful when you walk," she scolded. "You could easily trip over a hidden root."

Peter chuckled and pulled Charlotte to him as well. "He'll be fine, Charlotte."

"Mother, watch me!" Myla called. They watched as Myla aimed her arrow at the target and shot straight and true. Once again, the arrow sank into the red center.

"Well, done, my girl," Charlotte praised. "Your skill has improved."

Arthur squirmed in Peter's arms and he set the boy down. He watched as Arthur approached Myla and clung to her leg. Myla set her bow down and hoisted Arthur up. "One day when you are old enough I will teach you to shoot like no other," Myla said, bouncing Arthur up and down. "We will be the finest archers in the land."

Peter smiled at his daughter's plan. It was amazing to think that Myla's life was at stake twelve years ago. Soon, after arriving from Perdita, Peter had called the Council together and convinced them to aid him in waging war against the emperor. As the war raged on, the emperor's men dwindled as did his money and supplies. Shortly afterwards he was killed in battle, leaving his army at Peter's mercy. Peter had agreed to spare their lives if they would work off their treacherous ways by building housing and stores for the people. If they refused to cooperate, Peter would hold an execution. Many took up his offer but some didn't. Their pride wouldn't let them see any way out of death. So, without any other option, Peter declared their deaths.

Now, after much work, Perdita was a new town and one of the grandest ports for ships to come to. They supplied Aurum with many new exotic goods and in return were given some goods from Aurum and protection from invaders.

Aurum had grown in size and was harder to rule, but with a strong-willed queen ruling beside him, Peter knew he could survive. He looked back at Myla letting Arthur examine her bow. Myla would be Aurum's protector until Arthur came of age. And, Peter knew, with his son and daughter as Aurum's protectors, the kingdom was destined to survive for many generations.

Made in the USA
Middletown, DE
06 January 2020